I0517065

VOLTAR THE LITTLE VAMPIRE

KORRA GREY

MOSS PENWORKS

Dedicated to my son John F. Stock (Doobie) and my grandson, Richard Alexander Stock. They are worthy of remembrance for the kindness and laughter they brought to others. Their lives were full of love, gentleness and appreciation for the great outdoors.

ACKNOWLEDGMENTS

I wish to thank my friends from The Quartz Hill Writers Club.

They encouraged me to write something so different from the novels still sitting on my computer. Thankfully, they suggested writing a short story or this book would never have happened.

I guess they figured I would never get a book out unless I did a short story first.

A special thanks to Briana who helped me put this whole thing together as well as Susie's encouragement while working on it. Lastly, Sonia, who helped me edit this book by asking so many questions I had to think about before answering them to make the book flow smoothly.

I appreciate you ladies so much and all your support.

Lastly, a special thanks to my granddaughters, Bella, Briana, Donnellan, Emily, and Katie Stock.

Thank you all.

CHAPTER 1

The Moving Book

E mily Paige, a freshman at a peaceful college, resembled a youthful Wonder Woman. She met Sebastian, a junior, while studying in the library only a month ago. She had an English assignment due the next day, and he offered his help.

'*Where is he?*' Emily thought, pushing a lock of her thick black hair behind her ear. They agreed to meet in the older study room of the library. He was late.

Sebastian arrived a short time later, wearing his usual ugly bow tie. He was a verifiable bookworm, complete with wire-frame glasses. A tiny paunch around his middle and his large build, added to his, 'bull in a china shop' image. She watched him placed a small folder of old school papers on the large study table, knowing that two years before, he aced the assignment she needed finished by tomorrow.

The library was almost empty. The teachers canceled all classes for the day to prepare for a play in the auditorium later that afternoon. Most students slept in, or left school for the holiday. Only the Library, Auditorium, and First Aid rooms remained open.

While Emily sat in a semi trancelike state, waiting for Sebastian to find his old assignment inside the folder, an older leather-bound book on the shelf tilted ever so slightly. The book moved again right before her eyes, completely breaking her trance. Emily blinked hard as her mouth dropped open.

The ancient writing on the old books binding flamed a soft golden glow!

The book wiggled on the shelf as if it were trying to release itself from its place between the other books before the glowing and movement suddenly stopped!

"Did you see that?" she whispered somewhat loud to Sebastian from across the table.

"Shush. Do you want to get us kicked out of the library, again?" he questioned.

With her eyes fixed on the book, she motioned for him to come closer with one hand as she patted the back of the chair next to her with the other.

Without a word, he picked up his books and moved. The smell of her sweet jasmine perfume filled his nostrils as he sat closer to her.

"Watch the thick old book on the third shelf in front of us," she said. "Tell me I'm not crazy. The book moved by itself!"

"What?" he questioned, squinting through his thick glass lenses at the shelf. A moment later, he spotted the movement as the book shifted and glowed again. His eyes rounded and his head shifted backwards in disbelief. His lips parted as if he wanted to say something.

She darted her eyes between him and the shelf and covered her mouth with one hand as the words on the books binding glowed once more.

Sebastian froze.

The lights above them flickered as they stared at each other.

"You must have seen it move that time," she whispered, grabbing his arm.

Lifting his eyebrows high above his glasses, he looked at her. "Yeah, I saw it," he said before raising his voice an octave. "Time to go!"

He began stacking up the books he had pulled out for the assignment. "I believe in signs. Books that move or glow, are not natural. It's a sign, Emily, that it's time to leave."

Twirling a lock of her long black hair, she continued to sit and stare at him. "Aren't you curious why?"

"Nope! Not at all; it's creepy and none of my business."

"Oh, Sebastian, maybe it's only a tiny mouse stuck behind it. If the library has mice, we need to tell someone. A mouse might chew the old books kept here and the library would lose them forever."

After fluttering her thick black eyelashes at him, she pleaded, "Don't be such a chicken. Please, go look."

"All right, stay here," he ordered as the lights flickered again.

As Sebastian trudged toward the shelf, he imagined himself marching toward some invisible guillotine. Adjusting his bow tie away from his throat with one finger, he swallowed. Holding his breath and closing his eyes, he reached out and pulled the mysterious book from the shelf.

Relieved to find no hidden creature on the shelf, he exhaled. As he held the ancient book with one hand, he turned around, raised his eyebrows, and shook his head as if to say, 'I told you so'.

"Bring it over here, I want to see it."

"Here's your spooky book," Sebastian said, walking over and dropping the book on the table with a thud. "There are no mice on the shelf moving it. The lighting in this room is bad; maybe the lights are playing tricks on our eyes."

She smiled as she entertained the thought they were the police investigating a great mystery. Her azure eyes sparkled with excitement. She loved to read the old Nancy Drew mysteries when she was younger, and this reminded her of one of them.

"Take my hand while I open the book; if there's a critter inside, I'll need back-up."

She cast a quick glance at Sebastian. "Are you ready?" she said, placing one hand on the book cover.

The book appeared ancient, fragile and worn. The title was impossible to read since it was in some language, neither knew.

"Ready," he responded, picking up a heavy dictionary lying on the table.

"Put down that dictionary Sebastian! If there's a mouse inside this old book, it's tinier than your hand. Now sit," she ordered and shook her head at him before shifting her eyes back to the book as he sat.

"Here goes." She edged the finger of her other hand inside the middle of the book, ready to open it.

A crackling sound of lightening broke through the silence in the room. The study room darkened while a golden glow spread over the edges of the entire book.

The book suddenly sprang completely open. She abruptly pulled her hands out of the way as it slammed against the table. Visible on the page was a colored, hand-drawn picture of a wooden coffin in an old barn. Included in the picture was a young boy walking out into a field at dusk.

Sebastian held his breath and leaned back. The front legs of the chair lifted off the ground as he pushed away from the table. His throat dried around his vocal cords as he attempted to tell Emily to close the book, but no words came out.

The illustrated picture of a boy changed before their eyes. The boy glided across the page. He appeared to be a young dark-haired vampire child from an old, scary story, complete with sharp, white fangs.

Emily blinked and sat back. Her lips parted in surprise.

The young vampire's whitish hand shot straight into the air and continued upward while his other hand followed above the page. His forearms emerged next. The higher the arms rose above the book, the larger they became until his whole body stood full size on top of the book, as a real person.

Stepping completely out of the book, the young vampire stared at her.

The book slammed shut on its own accord after the boy appeared, and the aura that surrounded it, vanished.

Emily glanced over at Sebastian whose face had turned white, as he promptly fainted, knocking the chair over as he fell onto the floor.

Confused, she tried to make sense of what just happened. *The boy cannot possibly be real. It must be a virtual reality game,* she thought. *Some version of a new 3D projection the library borrowed to put on display for Open House night. What harm can an illusion do?*

The little vampire looked to be about nine and dressed in sixteenth century garb. Brown knee-high pants with a white shirt and white socks, like hose, covered his legs below his knees. Large clunky shoes on his feet completed the look of an old century boy, except for the fangs above his bottom lip. He stood in front of them as a young lad from some long-ago era.

"I am Voltar; who are you, madam? What century is this, please? Since being locked inside that book, I have lost track of time," the vampire stated.

She mentally noted his thick English accent as he sat on the table and waited for her answer. Still convinced it was a game, she knew there had to be some instructions she should follow in order to play.

"My name is Emily. How do I play this game and how did you get inside the book?"

Voltar cast his gaze toward Sebastian on the floor. The vampire had no expression except a single raised eyebrow. "Your friend there," he said, tilting his head and shifting his eyes over to Sebastian, "is he, dinner, or dead? I am famished, dear lady."

"Neither!" she replied in a sharp tone. Alarmed by such a question from a game, she gave the room a quick scan for a hidden camera, before she bent over to wake Sebastian. After a nudging and a gentle slap to his face, she smiled when he opened his eyes.

"Ah-h-h . . . my . . . my blood sugar must have dropped," Sebastian said, sitting up and looking down to check for any injury to his body. He touched his wrist to take his blood pressure. "I had a hallucination. A strange vampire boy seemed to come out of that moving book on the table. It was positively a weird dream."

"To be certain, it is rather unusual I assure you, but about time," Voltar stated leaning over the edge of the table. "I found myself imprisoned inside that book far too long." The little vampire jumped off the table and glanced at the unfamiliar surroundings.

Sebastian leaned back as if he would faint again.

"Oh-h-h, no-you-don't!" Emily said, pulling at his shirt and helping him stand. "I believe this boy is one of those new interactive virtual reality games," she whispered. "I bet there's even a camera in here somewhere, recording us. Let's play."

"I hope not," he answered. A video of his fainting would make his life intolerable since the other students at the school already thought he was strange.

Voltar stared at Emily. With her fair skin and ebony hair, he assumed she must be a vampire as well. "Are you sure he is not dinner? By his size, he is large enough for both of us to have a feast dear lady."

"We'll talk about 'dinner' later. Now, how did you get locked inside the book?" To interact with this new game, she needed to know where to start.

"Well," he sighed, "Vampires live in my city. There were many stories of a witch who lived near Paupers Alley in London. I walked a few doors down from the bakery shop where my mother sent me for a loaf of bread, because they said a witch there sold charms of protection to halt the turning of one into a complete vampire. I went inside her shop, since I was newly turned that very night.

"Everything was fine at first, until I tried to convince the witch to give me the charm free, since I was just a boy and had no money. I thought she would feel sorry for me and give it to me gladly. She smiled and brought me to her back room and told me to wait as she put the proper spell on the charm she would freely give me.

"As I waited, I watched her smear the bloody thing with something that smelled of pig dung. She opened that book on the table," he said pointing to the ancient book, "and said I should place the charm inside my pocket. After assuring me, I would be safe from hunters of my kind; she said a few words and touched a blank page in the book. Afterwards, I found myself cast inside the book."

"Do you have the charm now?" Emily asked.

"Yes. I wiped all the dung off as soon as I arrived inside the book and placed the cursed charm on a stone, vowing never to touch it again. But alas, I found myself still trapped in that miserable book. I realized I might need the charm to leave that place. I have carried the stinky thing with me for centuries. It is here in my pocket."

Voltar pulled the piece from his pocket. "See, there is no

intelligent reason I remained a prisoner inside that book by this thing. The old witch must have cursed it, and me with it."

"May I inspect it?" Sebastian asked, holding out his hand and winking at Emily.

If the boy and his charm were holograms from a virtual reality game as they both suspected, its non-solid-form would prove neither one, beyond a doubt, existed.

Voltar dropped the enchanted charm into Sebastian's hand!

Emily and Sebastian stared at each other. The charm was solid, not a hologram. The vampire and the charm, with its obnoxious odor from the dung stuck in its crevices, were real.

"Not good," Sebastian said under his breath as he ran his other hand through his thick brown hair. The skin on the back of his neck tingled, as he turned a shade paler. "Not good at all."

"Now don't faint again," Emily whispered. "We have to figure this out."

"May we now eat lady?" Voltar inquired, giving his lips a slight lick. "I am feeling famished and weak. I have not had sustenance for centuries."

CHAPTER 2

Vampires are Hungry Creatures

"He's real, and he's hungry," Sebastian whispered in a high, 'sing-song' voice.

Emily's hand shook as she grabbed Sebastian's. She turned toward Voltar. "We need to discuss a quiet place for you to—dine." Moving closer to the door she added, "We'll be right over here."

Out of Voltar's hearing distance, she asked, "Is there a blood bank around here or, a place we can donate blood?"

"How about we just put him back in the book?" he whispered. "I can slip the charm into his pocket and—,"

"Let's see," Emily interrupted, smiling at him before she wrenched her hand free from his.

"First," she murmured while her eyes blazed into his, "He's hungry, NOW! He asked if you were dinner a minute before you woke up. Are you ready to be a snack for a vampire?" she added sarcastically. "He told us the witch smeared stuff on the charm before she imprisoned him inside the book. Even after he wiped it off, he remained stuck there! You heard him say that, right?"

"Yes, now that you mention it," he answered, upset with himself that he forgot. He was smart, and here he was acting like a mindless fool in front of her.

Emily glanced away to think. "First things first. We need to get 'vampire food' or his dinner will be us. We'll figure out later how to put him back in the book after he has eaten, or drank, or whatever. You've been here for two years; you must know some-place to get blood!"

"The first-aid room across from the auditorium next door!" he blurted out. "It's open for emergencies. Maybe they have blood there—,"

"Great idea!" she interrupted, taking a few steps back in Voltar's direction. "Just play along with what I tell the little vampire."

"Voltar," she said, "in this century we do things differently than the one you came from. Here, we have blood banks, as we call them, that supply blood to those of us in need. We need to go there to get you dinner," Emily said with a big smile.

"You can travel in the *sunlight* here?" Voltar questioned looking at the light filtering shades pulled across the windows. "It is still daylight; I cannot leave until night falls. How is it possible for vampires to leave before night?"

"That is a fine question." Emily hesitated to answer while her head tilted downward.

"Times have changed since your imprisonment inside that book, my young friend," stated Sebastian after giving Emily a side-glance. "It took a few centuries but, through science, we discovered a drug that allows us to walk about in the daylight. After the drug's discovery, there was no longer a need to fear the sun."

Emily's large azure eyes grew even larger at Sebastian's excuse. She nodded in approval and appreciation for his quick response. Sebastian wasn't a jock. He was skittish over things out of his control, but he was quick-minded and smart. She smiled as she stared at his pewter colored eyes behind his old-fashioned wire frames while he spoke. His soft speaking voice seemed to calm her.

"Sebastian and I will leave to find you 'sustenance'. You must wait here for your own protection. Read the books in here, but remember, our world differs from the one you left, so stay inside this room," Emily instructed the young vampire.

"Madam, please hurry. The witch who locked me inside the book will surely come looking for me. If you can though, bring me the drug your husband spoke of that allows me to go out into the sunlight. It has been centuries since I have felt the sun on my face."

"Call me Miss Emily and he is *not* my husband, he's my friend," she emphatically stated, surprised that the nine-year-old vampire thought such a thing.

"My mistake Miss Emily, you look far too mature and pretty not to be married by now." The vampire raised an eyebrow and then asked her, "Do you have the pox?"

Sebastian snickered and did his best to stifle a laugh as he looked at her.

Speechless by the vampire's question, her cheeks blushed as she took a small step backwards. Her eyes shot daggers at the two of them.

"You would make a fine marriage together. He may even be loyal to only you, considering he is so advanced in age and too old to have affairs," Voltar added with a side-glance at Sebastian.

Voltar gave a small sigh before he volunteered more information. "I was engaged at five to a lovely girl. We were to be wed at twelve. Alas, a vampire attacked me and I never saw her again. Surely she wed someone else."

"Voltar, we... or rather all of us here," Sebastian said, "live longer in this century and marry later in life."

"Really?" Voltar pondered, sounding quite surprised at the thought. "Strange," he murmured. "Are they able to perform their marriage duties with such frail bodies?"

Emily covered her mouth with one hand, hiding a laugh.

Sebastian, embarrassed by the boy's question, dropped his head and looked down at the ground. He remembered Voltar thought them to both be vampires like him and was not intentionally insulting him.

"Yes. We wait to have children until much older," Sebastian restated.

"Oh well, it does not concern me, but strange as it is, it is informative none the less. This new era is undeniably unconventional. I am wondering if I am still in the city of London, or is this Scotland by chance." Voltar asked.

"We are in the United States of America," Emily proudly stated. "This state is Maine, which is one of fifty states joined as one nation across the ocean from England."

"Oh! Others of my time have spoken of this savage new world. I have never visited here or gone on any voyage myself. It does not seem as primitive as I have heard."

"It was, 'primitive' as you say, a long time ago, but it has grown friendlier to our kind," stated Emily. "The books will tell you all about the history you have missed while you wait. The computers," she said pointing to the desks with computers lined up against the wall, "will also explain whatever you want to know."

"Computers?" Voltar asked, confused by what looked to him to be metal and glass boxes on desks.

"Ah, never mind those over there, look through the books instead," suggested Sebastian arching an eyebrow at Emily.

"I will wait until your return and enjoy looking at the books. In my time, we valued them and held them in high esteem. It is pleasant to know at least, *that,* has not changed," Voltar declared.

"It may take us a little time before we return so don't talk to anyone," Emily said. "In this century, it's hard to tell who may have a diet such as ours, and will be frightened of you."

"I understand. In my time, people were also frightened of our kind. They were cruel to the point of driving a stake through the hearts of those like us. I was fortunate being recently turned. None dreamed a boy would be a vampire."

"Yes, you were lucky," Sebastian stated. Under his breath, he murmured, "Lucky indeed."

"Just stay here until we get back, Voltar," Emily reminded him.

CHAPTER 3

Comfort

Voltar walked over to the window and gazed outside at his new surroundings after Emily and Sebastian. He felt a sudden blast of cool air wash over him. Looking up, he noticed a metal grate stuck in the ceiling above his head. Cool air blew down on him, but it appeared warm and sunny outside. *How very odd,* he thought.

A young female strolled into the study room, breaking his concentration on the grate. He watched her as she dropped the satchel she carried onto the long table in the center of the room. She opened the old leather-bound book Emily left on the table.

The lights in the room flickered again.

Voltar scrutinized the female's curious attire. She dressed in tight pants, like those that Emily wore. The women of his time never dressed in pants! Unusual as that was, the pants she wore appeared ripped in various places, and hardly covered her long legs. *She must be poor,* he determined. Continuing his inspection of her, her upper body clothing caught his attention the most.

How common and unladylike, he thought, though, but he

couldn't turn away. A snug fitting undergarment, of bright pink, barely covered her voluptuous bosom. The garment had sparkly things all over it and tiny, thin, red straps, which scarcely held up the top of the cloth.

Her hair was an unconventional color, a deep rich purple, pinned up haphazardly on top of her head. The female's bold face paint made her resemble some 'creature of the night'. Deep blue and red powder covered her eyelids in streaks, and it sparkled. A blackish-blue lipstick smeared across her lips while black charcoal pencil, such as actors used in the theater, outlined her eyes.

A black leather spiked collar, similar to an animal's choker, hung around her neck. It made him think she might belong to someone in this century. In his opinion, she was *uncommonly strange*.

In his estimation, she looked like a pet raccoon.

Voltar rubbed his eyes with his fists and looked again. Was she an animal who transformed, or a strange human of the times? She was in the wrong place to find others of her kind; he thought.

"Hello," she whispered. "Is this your book," she asked, opening the book and turning a page.

The sound of thunder echoed above as the room darkened. The book glowed for the second time.

Voltar grabbed the female's hand, pulling her off the chair and ran with her to the nearest door. Upon opening the door, his hand burned and blistered in the sunshine. Rapidly closing the outside door, he stood there for a moment realizing the door he picked led to outside. *That* was not an option.

He ran through the corridors of the library as he pulled her behind him, looking for another door. "Where are you taking me?" the female shouted at the boy.

Voltar ran across the library where he found another door.

Still clasping her hand firmly, he slowly opened the door. The room, filled with bright lights and no windows, gave him hope that they would be safe from the witch inside. Much to his shock, the room smelled like flowers, but there were no vases overflowing with them to account for the strong scent.

After pulling her inside, the female wrenched her hand from his.

"What are you doing, you crazy little boy?"

"Madame, I am trying to save your life."

"Save my life by taking me into the men's bathroom?" she asked, raising both eyebrows.

"Is this a bathing room? I see no tub." Confused, he added, "There is only the smell of invisible flowers in here."

"A tub? You think there should be a tub in here?" she questioned, ignoring the remark about the air fresheners.

"Well, you called this place a bathroom, did you not?" Voltar asked.

"It's the restroom, you little ignoramus."

"I see no beds. I see nothing in here except those little doors. Is that where the beds are?" he asked. "My name is Voltar and I am not from here. I do not know all your customs. What might your name be, miss, miss—?"

"My name is Vicky, and this," she said holding one of the stall doors open, "is the place where you, you know, use the facilities to relieve yourself." She stuttered and shook her head as she walked over to the sink.

Voltar followed her. "Thank you very much as I needed to relieve myself, some time ago. I will now use one of the tiny rooms with a door. I shall be only a few minutes."

Voltar walked past Vicky, who stood with her back to the mirrors above the three sinks. He strolled into one stall.

"Oh my," Voltar said, holding the stall door open. "It does not smell awful in here or look like the privy I am used to using.

It looks rather comfortable actually and smells like a field of flowers."

Vicky shook her head and turned toward the mirror behind her to check her make-up as Voltar walked into the little room. The boy had no image reflected in the mirror!

She slapped her hand across her mouth and then took the opportunity, as he went inside the stall, to run. She ran out the front door, not even stopping to tell the librarian about the strange boy without an image in the bathroom mirror.

Sitting inside the stall he stated, "It is a rare find this little room. Thank you for showing it to me. What is inside this big thing on the wall?" he asked.

No response.

"The stick sponges inside a bucket of salt-water, commonly used back home under these circumstances, are not in here. Vicky, is there something useful in this rectangular box mounted to the wall? How do you clean your exterior parts?"

Fiddling with a tiny slit on the bottom of the rectangular box, he felt a roll of paper inside. Stumped, he scanned the tiny room, attempting to figure out why there was a box with soft paper inside, but no bucket.

"Ah-ha!" he exclaimed after a minute. "I think I have figured out what the box and paper is for, and it is *not* for writing, there are no words on it," he declared.

Reaching inside the slit at the bottom, he tried to get at the paper, but it just rolled around. There was no end to the paper he could grab. Frustrated, he pulled the box off the wall.

After a minute of unrolling the paper inside the box, he triumphantly shouted, "I have released the paper from it! It is an exasperating experience to get the paper out of the box. The people of your century must devise some other way to get at the paper."

His words echoed off the walls. He thought it rude that she

made no response to his suggestion. "What do you think?" he asked, walking out of the stall.

"Vicky? Vicky, where are you? Are you playing hide and seek?" No response came. "Very well, I shall play the game and find you."

Voltar pushed open the first stall. No Vicky.

He checked every stall before realizing she had left. His stomach rumbled.

CHAPTER 4

The Plan

"Now to the First Aid room to get blood," Emily said, as they walked outside the library doors.

"I can't believe you, Emily. How can you remain so calm? There's a vampire, a small vampire, but a real vampire, waiting in the library and he's hungry on top of it! How, pray tell, is this *our* problem? Call the police and let them deal with him and his hunger."

"Oh, yeah, Sebastian, I'm sure that'll work. We tell them a vampire popped out of a book I was reading and um—what then? Order them to take care of the little vampire problem? Sure, they'll believe us, right?" she said dropping her voice. "It's more likely they'll cart us off to the local nuthouse," she ranted.

Sebastian raised his glasses above his hairline and rubbed his face with both hands in frustration, looking similar to one of the Three Stooges.

"How are *we* equipped to handle this, Emily?" he asked, putting his glasses back on. "That creature needs to feed before he goes out and grabs a person off the street. On top of that, we have no idea how to get him back in the book. He stands out like a sore thumb dressed in those mid-century clothes and speaking as if he just got off the boat. What's *your* plan?"

"Well, we're going to First Aid to get him blood before he turns us or anyone else into a vampire. We'll have more time to figure out how to get him back in the book after he eats," Emily said, walking faster.

"How do you suggest asking the woman who runs the First Aid room for blood? What are we going to say? We need blood for a friend. Are you crazy? She won't give us blood with a lame excuse."

"Good idea," Emily said. "We'll tell her a friend of ours is a bleeder and needs blood because he cut his arm or something. Let's just try."

Sebastian shook his head. He considered Emily fairly normal and pretty when they first met. He forced down the idea now creeping around in his mind, that she was off kilter and crazier than his mother and father. His parents had always acted strangely, whispering when they thought he was out of hearing distance. They did things unlike any other normal parents.

"Emily, you're as weird as my parents. You come up with ideas no other living person in the entire world would consider."

"You haven't seen weird parents until you've met my family," she responded. "My family presumes all other people are out to get them."

He was ready to walk away from her when she suddenly stopped and turned toward him.

"Sebastian," she said, staring into his eyes. "I'm so thankful you're here with me. What would I do without you?"

Then, giving him a quick kiss on the lips along with a friendly hug, she added, "I don't think I could handle this alone."

Her lips appeared to tremble as he gazed back at her. "Okay,

okay I'll help you," Sebastian said, as a flush of embarrassment colored his face from her kiss. The fragrant strawberry smell of her hair filled his nostrils. He fought wanting to leave her right then, but he couldn't walk away. She needed him no matter what she thought.

"But if he turns me into a vampire, you're the first one I'm going after," he stated.

She smiled as they continued toward the building where the first aid room was located.

Sebastian stopped for a moment, standing before the large metal doors of the newly modeled building. He hesitated as if he wanted to say something, then jerked the door open but declined giving a reason for his reluctance. A glisten of moisture materialized across his forehead and his hands felt clammy.

Walking in silence until reaching the first aid room, an older woman with glasses who sat at the desk, looked up.

"Sebastian, what's wrong with you now? I swear, you're the most chronic hypochondriac I have ever had the pleasure to meet," she stated putting down her pen on top of the paper she'd been filling out.

"Miss Montego," Sebastian began with a weak smile, all the while hoping Emily didn't hear what the woman behind the desk said. "We have an emergency. A friend, a fellow student who has hemophilia, has cut his arm and needs blood. I was afraid to move him. His bleeding might increase, so we're here to get blood to save his life."

The woman raised one eyebrow high above her glasses, scrunched her face together like a prune, and pursed her lips tightly while glaring at him. She gave no response. She bent her head down after a moment and went back to her paperwork, ignoring him.

Sebastian turned toward Emily, who nodded to continue.

"Miss Montego, this is an emergency!" Sebastian said

pounding a fist on the counter, attempting to sound and act more forceful.

"Mr. Liggett, call an ambulance if, and I say if, your friend is as you say, potentially bleeding to death." She stood up, giving him the one–eyed once-over complete with an arched eyebrow, for such a ridiculous request. "Young man, they do not equip us to handle such things here. Nor will I send for blood, no matter what dire need there may be. Call 911. Now, be on your way!"

Emily elbowed Sebastian in the ribs. "Let's go," she murmured.

Once outside, Emily sneered at him. "Are you crazy? You sounded like a whiney little boy who just dropped his ice-cream cone!"

"I did not!"

"Did too."

"Not."

"Never mind!" Emily howled. "We need to find blood. Is there another place people donate blood around here? You can donate a pint of blood and we'll take it back for Voltar."

"I'm not doing that! I need my blood," Sebastian said, alarmed by her suggestion. "It keeps my body functioning and— uh, my mind able to think," he added. "I'm not giving my precious blood to that vampire. My blood is part of me and a *part,* I intend to keep."

"Really Sebastian? Would you rather become a vampire's dinner and end up giving all of your blood as an offering to Voltar? I'm sure he'd think you'd be quite tasty and filling too."

Sebastian stopped. He focused on the trees across the path while he considered her words. Catching back up to her, he rubbed his hands together before speaking.

"There's a blood bank over on Tenth Street. People donate blood over there all night. I—," he dragged out, "don't have enough blood. I think you should be the one to donate blood instead. You're the one who opened the book and let him out."

Emily halted in mid-stride. Her mouth dropped open before clamping shut. She said nothing but began to walk faster, stomping her feet with each step.

"We need to hurry," Emily yelled back as she cut across the grass. "We've left him alone in the library for a long time, and he needs blood. It's not safe to leave a hungry vampire alone when dusk is setting in."

"The donation center is just around the corner," Sebastian said. "Has anyone ever told you Emily, you're opinionated and pushy?" he mumbled from behind her.

Emily smiled and continued walking.

CHAPTER 5

Sir Knight Sebastian

The donation center looked more like an old deserted building than a sanitary clinic. With paint peeling off the door and graffiti sprayed on the crumbling brick walls, Emily questioned if they were at the right place. She saw a sign hanging on the window and a faded red cross painted on the door. The sign read; 'Blood Bank. Walk right in'.

"What's your plan this time Emily?" Sebastian asked. He smiled noticing she appeared a little green after seeing the dilapidated building.

Emily fidgeted with the collar of her blouse and then chewed on her nails before answering. "Well, we'll tell them we're here to give blood, and the moment we go into the back room with the nurse, we'll grab some blood and run."

Sebastian chuckled as he looked down and folded his hands across his thick chest. "To be allowed into the area where they store the blood Emily, you must donate some. Are you sure, you want to do this? We could always find a pointed piece of wood to use as a stake, and get rid of Voltar altogether. He'd just disappear. There, problem solved."

"He's just a boy Sebastian. That would be cruel. It's not his fault someone turned him into a vampire. We're getting him some blood, end of story. I'll do the talking this time."

"And you will donate the blood, right?" he questioned again before he declared, "not me."

"Whatever, scaredy cat," she huffed, grabbing the door handle as she swung it open for him to go in first.

As they stepped inside, the stench of blood was overwhelming. The nauseating smell made Sebastian want to run from the place. He could almost taste it as he ran his tongue over the inside of his mouth.

Emily noticed that the inside of the building appeared worse than the outside. Two men, who looked like bums, sat in grimy white plastic patio chairs along the dirty wall. A gray, threadbare rug, that seemed at least forty years old from its appearance, covered the floor. One chair, turned upside down and laced with cobwebs across its legs, stood in the center of the large waiting room.

Emily walked up to the glass partition at the nurses' station while Sebastian stood near the door. A male attendant standing a short distance behind the glass partition, shuffled over to her. He was an older man with a scruffy beard. His clothes smelled and looked like he got them out of a dumpster.

"Yes, what do you want," he croaked between having a long coughing fit. His unkempt straggly gray hair dangled around his bent shoulders as he hacked and spit phlegm into a nearby cup.

Emily rubbed her forehead, wishing she were anywhere but there. "We're here to donate blood," she offered. "Is the nurse available? I'd like to speak with her first."

"I'm the nurse, little lady," he said, leering at her while holding a clipboard with dirty papers on it. "I'll be right with you. These other two can wait," he added, nodding at the two men in the lobby. Another coughing fit grabbed the words he was about to add.

Emily waved her hand below the solid part of the partition while smiling at the man and motioned for Sebastian to come over. Frantic for him to get beside her, she waved faster.

The man watched as Sebastian strolled over to her. "No one can go back there but the one giving blood and the one taking it," the man barked at her.

"He's my brother," Emily said. "I have a tendency to faint and need him with me. Since you're a male, I'm sure you understand a female should not be alone with a male who is not family, under HIPAA guidelines." She didn't know if it was true or not, but felt he wasn't aware of the guidelines either by the looks of him, and it sounded good.

The old man grumbled but buzzed both of them into the backroom and handed her the clipboard he was holding for her to fill out. The room appeared dirtier than the reception area. Emily tried to remember if she recently had a tetanus shot.

She gave the clipboard to Sebastian to hold when she sat in the cracked leather chair. She shuddered as she noticed stains of old dried blood on the arm of the chair. When the man pulled the cart of supplies over to her and began to drain her blood, she closed her eyes, and prayed.

After pulling two bags of her blood, the old man walked over to the refrigerated glass cabinet against the wall, almost throwing the bags of her blood inside.

"I'll wait here, while you finish the paperwork and rest for a minute. Let me know when you're finished," he said turning his back on them. He put the used supplies in a garbage container and lit a cigarette.

Sebastian noted when the man stuffed the two bags of Emily's blood inside the refrigerator. Sebastian nudged her arm and shifted his eyes toward it. Her eyes followed his gaze, and she nodded.

"May I have a glass of water sir?" she asked.

"I have to go to the lunchroom to get a glass. Just stay here, I'll be right back," he said having another coughing seizure as he walked away.

Sebastian opened the refrigerator as soon as the man left and grabbed the two bags of blood. Emily jumped up from the chair and they ran out the front door never filling out the paperwork.

When they were a block away, they stopped running and began laughing.

"I can't believe we just did that!" Emily said still giggling.

"I'm a straight-A student," Sebastian cried getting serious. "If we get caught, my dad will kill me," he whined.

"Oh come on now, it was fun, but we better get back to our little vampire," she said walking toward the library. The campus grounds were only a short walk away.

She and Sebastian walked back to the library's study room. The room was empty.

"Voltar, where are you?" she whispered.

He said he was hungry, she thought.

"Check the whole library for him, or any bodies," she shouted running out of the room.

They scoured the private study rooms, the libraries aisles of books, and the halls, both upstairs and downstairs. No Voltar anywhere.

"Okay, we found no dead bodies, and that's good, but where would he go?" Emily murmured to Sebastian as ended their hunt in the middle of the library.

"You'll give me a heart attack," he huffed, flopping down in a chair next to where they stood. "Let's just leave and call the police. We'll tell them there's a lost boy on the grounds. After us stealing blood for the vampire who's flown the coup, I'm done."

"The bathrooms!" Emily shrieked. "We haven't checked them! Come on," she said, pulling him up from the chair.

Sebastian shuffled behind her to the corner of the library where the bathrooms were. He sat in a chair outside the bathrooms while she went inside the ladies' room.

"He's not in there. Check the men's room, Sebastian; he has to be in there. We've searched the whole library and he can't go outside. He's got to be in there."

"He might have left," he said, taking his pulse again. "Hopefully he has," he muttered under his breath.

Emily closed her eyes and shook her head slightly.

"What?" he questioned lifting his hands. "Am I wrong to hope?"

Behind the men's room door, they heard Voltar's voice. "Is that you?" he called out from inside the bathroom.

"You who?" Sebastian questioned, with a smirk on his face.

"Sebastian, cut it out," Emily reprimanded, giving him a dirty look. "Voltar is anyone in there with you," she asked hoping the little vampire hadn't drained the blood of someone who had to use the facilities.

"No, just me," he whispered.

"Go get him," Emily said, pulling Sebastian up from the chair and pushing him inside the door.

After a minute, Sebastian came out, alone. "Voltar won't leave. Your vampire said something escaped out of the book. He refuses to leave the bathroom."

"That's just silly. He's a little boy and probably imagining it because this is a new world that he's not used to. Give me the blood and tell him, when he's hungry, I'll have it in the study room. When he's hungry enough, he'll come out."

"Can't you just tell him through the door? He looked hungry in there and I don't want to end up his dinner if he's mad at *you*."

"No! Tell him what I said."

Sebastian turned a pale color and sat back down.

"Oh for goodness sakes, I'll do it," she said.

Emily threw the door open and grabbed Voltar by the hand. "Come with me," she commanded dragging him out of the bathroom and marching him back to the study room. Sebastian followed a short distance behind.

Voltar eyes darted throughout the study room the moment they stepped inside.

"Something came out of the book when Vicky turned the page. I don't know what, because we ran out the door to the facilities and stayed there, but it's in here somewhere," Voltar said sounding frightened. "It might be the witch."

"Who's Vicky? A witch?" they asked in unison.

"Oh, she's a very nice creature of the night, with purple hair. She came with me into the bathroom, but she left while I was in the little room with a door."

"Stop! I don't want to hear anymore about you and your —'creature of the night'!" Emily shouted gritting her teeth.

"Is she your friend?" asked Voltar, avoiding eye contact with her while she was in such an emotional state.

Throwing the bags of blood on the table, Emily quietly fumed and didn't bother to answer his question. "Have dinner," she ordered, "while Sebastian and I think of what to do next."

Someone in the back of the study softly began humming.

Emily cast Voltar a quick look before she and Sebastian stared at each other. Her eyes broke away from Sebastian's first, glancing over to the main aisle of bookshelves. "We'll be right back Voltar. We're just going to get a book, come on Sebastian."

Out of the vampire's hearing, she whispered to him. "Could

something else have escaped the book? Could it be the witch Voltar spoke of?"

"It was probably some student he didn't see come in. We're in a small town in Maine Emily, known for its old witch trials, but this is the eighties. There are no witches, werewolves, or vamp—,"

"No vampires?" she asked casting a quick glance at Voltar. "Let's just make sure, shall we?" she said pushing him in front of her down the main aisle of books.

"Why do I have to be the brave one," he murmured, just loud enough for Emily to hear, while refusing to move forward.

"Because, oh brave soul, you're my 'knight in shining armor'. Sir Knight Sebastian always saves the day," she smiled back, and then shoved him forward again.

"Can't I just be the court jester instead?" Sebastian asked stumbling forward.

CHAPTER 6

The Witch

As Emily and Sebastian walked down the main aisle in the study room, row upon row of bookshelves lining the room smelled of old paper and ink from an era gone-by.

They tiptoed through the larger center aisle to investigate where the humming came from and who was doing it. The sound grew louder as they approached one row ahead of them half-way down the aisle.

Sebastian froze. Emily grabbed his arm and pivoted behind him after giving him a slight push from behind, into the next row.

A woman, dressed in a fashionable gray suit, stood with her back toward him as he stumbled into the row. Hearing someone behind her, she swiveled her head a hundred-and-eighty degrees around, as if it were a normal movement.

She appeared to be in her late forties with black hair tied in a knot behind her head. The gray suit matched a streak of gray in the front of her hairline. Her appearance made him think she looked like an old schoolmarm.

Maybe she was a teacher, but he never saw her at school or around town before, and it was a small town. Was she the witch as Voltar suggested, or just an out-of-towner visiting?

Her heart-shaped face with high cheekbones caught his attention. The woman's eerie green, almost glowing eyes, pierced into his. He took a small step backward and bumped into Emily.

"Excuse us," Emily said, stepping out from behind Sebastian, while elbowing him in the arm. "We didn't know anyone else was in here."

"I'm sorry; I seem to have frightened you, my dears. I'm here looking for a young boy who I've, 'misplaced,'" she cackled in an old English accent. "Have you seen one?"

Sebastian shifted his weight on each foot, rocking back and forth before Emily spoke.

"Yes. Yes we did," she stated. "He's in the row, all the way in the back of the room," she added, clearing her throat.

"Thank you," the woman said, moving out of the aisle. However, as she passed Emily she waited a second, gazing at her a moment before moving on. The older woman appeared to glide, not walk, toward the last aisle.

"Come on, Sebastian," Emily whispered before rushing over to where Voltar was feasting.

"Your witch *is* here, let's go," she said to Voltar, grabbing the other bag of blood off the table he didn't finish. "Voltar, it's dusk, can you go outside now?"

"Yes," he answered.

Emily gripped his hand and rushed him toward the exit. She ran out the front door while Sebastian trailed behind them.

"Where are we going?" he asked, catching up to her.

"To the auditorium in the next building, There's a play going on for 'Back to School Night' with plenty of people inside. We'll get lost in the crowd."

After entering the auditorium, Sebastian took Emily by the hand, "I have an idea; just follow me."

The lights in the auditorium dimmed as the performance began. Sebastian led them behind the stage where the stage crews were bustling around. He ushered them into a room filled with a variety of costumes.

"Emily, find some clothes that Voltar can change into. He smells like a stable hand, and if I can smell him, the witch can too. She'll be able to track us by following his scent no matter where we hide. I'll keep a look-out while you get him into something without that awful odor or make him stand out like the absurd clothes he's wearing."

Sebastian hurried to the backstage curtain and stood near where the actors went on stage. His eyes were on the auditorium doors when they opened and the witch walked inside.

"Not good," he murmured, raising his eyebrows above his glasses. He hurried back to the prop room, while checking his blood pressure on his wrist along the way.

"The witch is here. Has he changed yet?" he asked, bursting into the room.

Voltar came out from behind the dressing divider, in clothes obviously three sizes too big.

"I do not think these fit properly," Voltar said, while trying to roll up the sleeves and hold up the pants at the same time.

Emily laughed at the boy. Sebastian shook his head before he turned and studied the costume rack.

"Throw on one of these costumes in here, Emily, over your clothes. When we were in the library, that witch stared at you longer than she did me, I'd like to know why. It'll change our appearance," Sebastian told her while grabbing a shirt off to put on off the rack.

"Put the boy's old smelly clothes inside the plastic bag over there on the chair. With a bit of luck, we may get past her without her spotting us. My car is right behind this building. Hurry!"

She grabbed a large old dress off the rack of costumes and smelled it before putting it on over her clothes. Sebastian peeked out the door, ready to leave.

"She's back here checking the dressing rooms!" he said.

Through the crack in the door, he watched the witch walk inside the room across the hall. "Ready, let's go," he said. He grabbed her hand while she clutched Voltar's.

They left the auditorium through the back door, running to the car. Emily pushed Voltar inside the back seat of the old car and slammed the door shut before getting in the front seat with Sebastian.

"Get the car started; she's coming out the door!" Emily shrieked, watching out the side window as the witch glided toward them.

He shook putting the key in the ignition and started the car. The witch suddenly appeared five feet in front of the car, preventing their escape as a mist formed around her. Sebastian sat paralyzed.

Voltar glared out the glass windshield as the witch's eyes glowed. She pointed her finger at him. The little vampire trembled, sinking down into the seat.

"Go!" Emily shouted. "Gun the engine!"

Sebastian shook his head as he cleared his trance-like state after Emily yelled. Suddenly slamming the car's gear stick into drive, he jammed his foot on the accelerator all the way to the floor. Four smoking tires squealed before taking off on the cement pavement. The car lunged forward.

The initial force of the car's movement jolted Emily and Voltar, slamming them against the back of their seats as Sebastian sped forward. Their heads hit the roof of the car as he plowed right over the witch!

Sebastian continued driving at a wild pace until they reached the forest preserves, five miles down the road. Out of immediate danger, he parked the car in a wooded area and promptly turned white.

"I've just killed someone! What if she wasn't a witch? Maybe she was only some innocent person. I'll go to jail!" Sebastian moaned while a gnawing feeling overwhelmed his senses as he relived the incident in his head. His hands tightly gripped the steering wheel as he dropped his head on top of his hands. "I'll spend the rest of my life in jail," he mumbled.

"Imagine that," Voltar volunteered from the back seat with a smile. After a moment he added, "This is a tin box that has comfortable seats and wheels." Voltar smiled before adding, "And it moves without horses!"

Emily shook her head, ignoring Voltar's assessment of the car.

"Emily, I have issues with high-stress situations. I don't know if I can handle any more of this."

"Do not worry, Sebastian," Voltar offered somberly. "She *is* the witch, and she is not dead. Your car, as you called it, only stopped her for the moment, but she will arise. We cannot kill her."

"What?" Sebastian and Emily said, turning their heads around looking at the vampire sitting behind them.

CHAPTER 7

How to Kill a Witch

"There is no way that I know of, to kill her," Voltar flatly stated.

"Explain," Emily demanded. "In great detail."

"When I first arrived inside the book, I spoke to those already imprisoned there by her. They told me she came many times before, and each time they tried to kill her. All of their attempts ended unsuccessfully. They said she cannot die."

"How about drowning her? There's a lake close to here," Emily suggested.

"That will not work. She just floats to the surface and smiles," Voltar said.

"What if we tied her to a tree and set her on fire?"

"That has been tried already. It did not work because she used her magic to break the ropes that bound her and blew out the fire," Voltar said and slumped down in the seat.

"Miss Emily, we endeavored to chop off her head, which ended with her scaring half of the town's people she put there. She ran around headless while holding her head in her arm as she chased us laughing wickedly until she eventually reattached it back on her shoulders. We tried other sorts of nastier ways, but failed. It appeared to be a game she enjoyed playing."

"Well, someone locked her inside that book and I'd like to know who and how," Emily said as she crossed her arms and flopped back against the seat.

"Something happened recently," Voltar offered. "She has not departed from the Book, since a few days ago. Perhaps a wizard cast her inside, I do not know. It is justice that she may have the same fate as those she imprisoned on the pages of the Book. I for one am glad, and feel no sorrow for her," Voltar smugly added.

"Voltar, do you know of any wizards?" Emily asked.

"No. I do not. I have only heard of them," the boy answered.

"What can she do besides glide?" Sebastian questioned. "That would be helpful to know."

"I really do not know the answer to your question, or why she is chasing me," Voltar said. "There were many of us inside the book and I am nothing special to her. I suppose she wants to keep us around to terrorize us."

"What are we supposed to do, keep on running?" Sebastian asked.

"That is what I would advise," Voltar stated matter-of-factly, nodding his head in agreement. "She will not stop looking for me. That is for sure."

"The stake idea is sounding better all the time," Sebastian murmured, looking out the car's window. "Are there any Poplar trees around here?" he mumbled, gazing up at the compact trees bunched together across from where he parked the car.

"Sebastian, cut it out. That witch will want us locked in her book or worse, since you ran over her with the car."

"You told me to!" Sebastian barked back. "It's your fault I ran her over, you and your little vampire friend there. I told you not to open the book. But, did you listen? No, and now we have a witch after us too," he groaned.

Emily scratched at her neck while Sebastian complained. The costume from the prop room irritated her skin. She pulled off the garment and threw it out the car's side window.

"So what do you want to do? We can't spend the night parked in these woods."

"I don't know."

Sebastian's stomach rumbled loud enough for her to hear it. "I didn't eat this morning and I'm hungry. I can't think of any options when my stomach cries out for food."

"Well, we can't go back to the school campus with that witch running around." Taking a glance at the gas gauge, Emily said, "Let's go to a gas station, get some gas, grab some foodstuff and I'll think on the way," Emily said.

"You can go out in the sun *and* eat food?" Voltar asked, wide-eyed and open-mouthed. "You must get me that potion."

Emily lowered her head and folded her hands in her lap without answering him while she thought.

Her parents' farm was fifty miles away. They should be safe there. She considered stoic father would not be happy at their arrival. He would be distant at first and act overprotective, but eventually warm-up.

"We're going to my parents' home," she announced, "until we figure out what to do. My parents have a farm in the country near here. We'll be safe there. But we need to get Voltar some civilized clothes first," she said, looking at his oversized attire.

"I have to call my mom!" Sebastian stated, sitting straight up and arching his back against the car's seat.

"What?"

"If we die, I have to tell her I love her, and my dad, too. I can't die without telling them that first."

"Voltar, go pick some flowers please, while I talk to Sebastian," Emily commanded. After the boy got out of the car, Emily turned toward Sebastian.

"Okay, call them. And don't forget to tell them about our little vampire problem. I'm sure that'll make their day. Oh, and I'd like to hear what you have to say about the witch chasing us." A sideways smirk appeared on her lips as she held up her hand and studied her nails while waiting for his answer.

"Never mind," Sebastian sighed, giving in to her logic.

Emily understood his desire, but the best way to handle his concerns, in her opinion, was to remain firm and concentrate on the matters at hand and not on feelings. She stuck her head out the car window and called for Voltar to come back.

Sebastian slowly turned the key in the ignition after the boy got back in the car and turned toward Emily, "Are you sure your parents will be okay with us dropping in for the night?" he asked changing the subject. "They'll know something is off since we have school tomorrow."

"They'll be too happy seeing me to squabble about missing a day of classes. Now drive!" she commanded. She knew her father might not be happy upon their arrival, since he was the one who pushed her to leave for college. He was a stoic man, but he loved her in his own way.

Sebastian put the car in drive. "Okay. After I drop the two of you off to get some clothes, I'll get some food and gas, then pick you up afterwards. I strongly suggest that we hurry and get on the road before that witch finds us."

"I'll tell my parents that Voltar is your little brother. My brother Zachary will enjoy having someone his own age to play with," she said, surprised by her own plan.

"I am a little old to play soldiers or whatever game it is that they play now," Voltar said indignantly.

"Voltar, you will play whatever my brother wants to play, is that clear? I'm not going to tell anyone you're a vampire who's centuries old," Emily told him.

Driving away from the preserves, Sebastian turned toward Emily. "Something's been nagging at me. How do we get the witch back in the book, if we left the book in the library? Did you figure *that* one out?" he smugly asked. "Don't you think we should we go back and get it?"

Emily raised an eyebrow and tilted her head to look at him. "No, not yet."

CHAPTER 8

The Arrival

"I will destroy them!" the witch vowed as she struggled to get up from the ground, but failed.

Terribly mangled from the car driving over her, she couldn't move her head. Her neck was broken. Casting her eyes over her body as she laid there, blood poured into one eye, she —smiled.

Her salvation was in her powers. Mumbling an incantation she used many times in the past, it began the slow process. The healing started with the gashes on her head.

Her neck's healing came next. The pain of healing caused her to grimace as the bones in her neck moved back into place. That accomplished, she raised her head and scanned the rest of her body. Flattened under the weight of the car, every bone in her chest lay crushed before her eyes. She felt the tortuous mending of her ribs as they expanded over the organs locked within. It took minutes that seemed like painful hours, to heal her torso completely.

A leg bone had shot up through the skin like a broken tree

branch. Looking at the wound, she saw tendons ripped apart and pulsating against the bone, while the adjoining muscles appeared filleted in pieces, like a fish.

All she could think of was how long it would take to heal. As she healed, thoughts of the boy's escape flooded her mind. Her pain-filled body was a burning throbbing pain she must endure for the moment pushing thoughts of the boy out of her mind. She put herself in a trance, easing the pain until the healing was finished.

The other leg, twisted beyond recognition, would come next. A deep cut on her arm exposed muscle and bone through an enormous gash. When her healing was complete, a pool of blood covered the area.

She stood after the healing had been accomplished, brushing herself off. Smudges of dirt, along with tire marks and crushed leaves, covered her clothes. By the time her body had repaired itself, the boy and those with him had disappeared without a trail to follow. She felt a loss of power.

Using her powers to heal herself had depleted a considerable amount of what little she had left. She spotted a large raven sitting in an evergreen tree nearby. Not wanting to deplete her dwindling powers, she called out to the raven.

"Find them and report back to me where they've gone," she commanded the bird.

The bird flew from tree to tree along the road, following the group to the preserves. He flew above the trees when they parked the car, before it flew back to the witch.

Upon the ravens' return, she again ordered the bird. "Take me to them."

The witch lifted off the ground. She flew after it a few feet before suddenly dropping to the ground. Bewildered, and taken aback by the loss of continuous flight, she tried again. This time, she only rose a few inches into the air before landing facedown on the dirt.

"My powers are dwindling! I can no longer fly! All was fine until that wizard came into my shop. How was I supposed to know he was a wizard? I only kept one blasted coin from his change when he cast me into the book, as if I had committed a great wrong.

"That wizard showed me my future if any of the ones I cast inside the book escaped. I followed the boy out of the Book to bring him back, but I have only three days to find him or the wizard will return to end me. It's all that devious boy's fault, I must return him to the Book. I will continue to lose my magic as each day passes. Then I will die a horrible death.

"At least I had my powers in the Book. But now, I have already lost the power to fly, and it is only the first day," she whined looking up at the raven. "I will follow you on foot if I must to find the boy!"

The bird flew above her as she walked.

The spell she used on her clothing upon her arrival became too restrictive. The high heels were uncomfortable and impossible to walk any distance in. After stumbling along the path for a quarter mile, she canceled the spell on her clothes and changed into her usual comfortable attire, a loose flowing black gown along with shoes fit for walking.

With the spell on herself canceled, her appearance changed back into what she really looked like. Her hair now, white and thin, hung on her shoulders like a disarrayed spider-web. Her body, bent in age, shortened and slumped over as the hump on her back returned.

She grumbled to herself as she went, "I must find the boy and leave this cursed place or it will be my doom." Grabbing a long stick on the ground, she used it as a cane to help her walk.

After the five-mile walk, she arrived at the forest's edge, and night had already set in. Sweaty and hot upon her arrival while wishing for a cool drink, she sat on a bench near the parking lot, to think and cool off.

"How were they able to travel this far? Even the fastest of horses could not have gotten them here in such a short time. Without my full powers, catching that boy seems impossible. The two super witches must be protecting him."

Glancing at the woods and surrounding area, she saw something shimmering on the ground in the moonlight. The witch walked over to the bundle of clothes the group left after taking them off. She picked up the discarded dress Emily wore and smelled the neck of the garment. It smelled of sweet perfume.

"Good. I at least have that girl's scent on the first day," she said to the raven sitting in a tree above her. "I will make those witches suffer for their meddling and sticking their noses in my business. It doesn't concern them; the boy is to be put back into the Book and now, *them* with him."

"I may no longer have all my powers, but with a little help I'll be able to track them. It will take more time than I thought, but I will find them."

Walking further into the forest, she expected to find a wolf or any kind of larger creature within the wooded area for her use. Disappointed at not even finding a wild boar roaming the area; she silently hoped to find a stream. Woodland animals always need to quench their thirst.

"There isn't even a puddle of water anywhere," she grumbled after a few minutes of searching the woods. "What kind of forest is this? There is nothing here but trees. Are there no animals in this land? What do the people here eat?"

A little chipmunk scrambled across her foot.

"Is this the only animal here? I guess it will have to do."

She picked up the chipmunk and held Emily's dress to its nose. "Find the one who wore this dress and lead me to her," she said holding the chipmunk by the back of the neck, "or I'll turn you into a toad!"

The little animal quivered in obvious fear as she held it above the ground. She tore the top of the dress off and put it in her pocket in case the chipmunk lost the scent. As the nightly mist rose, the chipmunk guided her through the back woods.

The witch climbed over logs, through high grass and patches of thorny bushes as she followed the chipmunk who easily hopped over or under the obstacles through the forest.

When she came upon a poor sighted, aged, and boney-looking deer who wandered nearby, she stopped. Between the deer's lack of good vision and his almost non-existent hearing, the witch walked over to him. The chipmunk scrambled away, running into a hole in the ground, safely hidden from her sight.

Holding the swatch of cloth up to the larger animal's nose, she commanded him to follow the scent and climbed upon his back. It was slow going, but at least she didn't have to walk over hills and dead tree stumps. They walked through the night.

CHAPTER 9

The Farm

Emily directed Sebastian through the winding country roads to her parent's farm, after they left the single-lane highway. The old sawmill was whining in the distance as they got closer to her parents farm.

Filled with excitement when they pulled in front of her home, she struggled getting the car door open in anticipation of seeing her parents. In that instant, she forgot about Sebastian, Voltar or the witch. A dimpled wide smile filled her face.

Her mother ran to greet her with a long warm hug. Emily's father followed behind his wife at a normal pace. With a sideways glance, he raised one eyebrow and glared at Sebastian, as he approached to greet his daughter.

Sebastian and Voltar stood by the car while Emily greeted her parents.

Beads of sweat broke out across Sebastian's forehead under her father's intense glare. "Lovely place to hold a Spanish Inquisition," Sebastian murmured between his teeth in an almost soundless tone, as he stood by the car. He flashed a quick but weak smile at the man.

Emily was thankful to be able to see her family since she'd never been away from home before leaving for college. She felt a twinge of sadness that her mother and father had no other family members to help with the farm at harvest time. They had led a quiet solitary life on the farm, having no company even when she was a young child. Bringing someone to the farm was an unusual experience for them.

"Mom, let me introduce you to my friends. The big guy over there is Sebastian, a schoolmate, and this is his younger little brother, Voltar," she said ushering Sebastian and the boy closer before placing a hand on the vampire's shoulder. Moments after the introductions were complete; she took her mother's hand and walked on the narrow path up the hill toward her family's older farmhouse. Sebastian and Voltar strolled at a slower pace behind her.

"Sebastian, I knew someone like you in the past, smart in a crisis," her father announced walking behind the group. "Emily, why did you bring your friend from school," Mr. Paige asked sounding somewhat cautious about the strangers coming to the farm.

"Well, he offered to drive, and I thought seeing an actual farm might be nice for his little brother," she said nonchalantly over her shoulder. "Zak will have a boy his own age to spend time with." Reaching the porch step, she turned to her mother, "Mom, you don't mind do you? They'll be no trouble."

"Of course not my dear, but a call first would have been nice so I could tidy up a little," she said pushing a loose stray hair back into the bun she wore while dusting off her dress.

"Mom, you look fine," Emily said giving her an extra hug. Her mother and father were still young looking, but a bit old fashioned in her opinion. The house smelled like fresh flowers and the home baked bread she committed to memory before leaving for school.

Her home looked exactly as she remembered, perfect. The smell from the kitchen told her beef stew was cooking on the stove. They always served dinner after dark on the farm.

Zak, her little brother, hearing her voice from upstairs, ran into the living room.

"Sis," he said running into her arms. "Boy, have I missed you."

"Zak, I want you to meet someone," Emily said while he gave her his impression of a bear hug. "This is Voltar, Sebastian's little brother," she added removing his arms from around her as she turned toward Voltar. "He'll be here until we leave tomorrow or the next day."

"So-o-o, this young man is your younger sibling. Am I correct?" Voltar asked in his strong English accent.

Emily saw Zak beam at the word 'man' the vampire used to describe him while her mother and father looked at each other, obviously surprised by the vampire's accent.

"Yes—yes he is," she answered as the room went quiet. "I know you were raised in England by your father, so our customs may seem somewhat different," she prattled on, afraid to stop. "Our lifestyle on the farm is quiet, but boys are boys everywhere," she said giving her mother a wide smile while ruffling Voltar's hair.

She watched Sebastian hold his breath as she attempted to make an excuse for Voltar's unusual accent to her parents. The air suddenly felt as thick as a blanket to her.

"Yes. After my father and mother divorced, my father moved there and raised my younger brother," Sebastian added.

"Voltar is precocious and he's even enrolled in advanced classes. He has a larger than normal vocabulary and reads more than many others of his age. He's into being proper at this stage, almost like someone from another century," he said, giving a weak half-hardy chuckle. "At least that's what my father said after talking with his teachers. My father sent him here to be with us for a short vacation," Sebastian rambled on.

Emily raised her hand and drew it across her throat while giving Sebastian the evil eye. "Mom, can I help you with dinner?" she asked changing the subject.

"It's all finished dear. Please, just set the table and we'll eat," her mother answered, walking into the kitchen.

Voltar pulled Emily aside into the dining room while Sebastian conversed with her father a short time.

"I cannot eat food, or drink even water," the young vampire said. "If I try to eat, I will heave it out at once! Your parents will notice when I throw-up or do not eat. What do you wish me to do?"

"I'll make some excuse for you. Just go talk to my brother." As an afterthought she added, "Be nice. Don't tell him anything about yourself. Get him talking about the farm and what he likes to do."

"Mom," she called out, "Voltar is on a special diet and can eat only special food. He's had a long day and his stomach is a wee bit upset. Can he go lie down in Zak's room on the spare bed?"

"Sure, but he should try to have at least some warm milk, it might help his stomach," she answered. "You were never sick as a child; we made sure of that, not even a broken arm or anything," her mother beamed, as if a broken arm was normal for most children.

"I know, you kept me in a pillow of love," Emily said teasingly. "Voltar's lactose intolerant mom, the milk would only make his stomachache worse," she quickly stated, making the saddest-looking face at her mother she could conjure up.

"I'll go upstairs and settle him in Zak's room. After he's all settled, I'll come down for dinner."

Emily walked over to Voltar who was standing next to Zak and touched his forehead. "I can see you're not feeling well. How about we go upstairs and skip dinner? I'll put you to bed where you can rest from that long trip to America."

Disappointment flushed over Zak's face, as relief rushed over Voltar's.

"Can't we play at least a short time before he has to go to bed?" Zak asked.

"You'll have a full day of play tomorrow, after chores," Emily reminded him and hurried the vampire upstairs.

Voltar's eyes rounded when he walked into Zak's room. Plastic dinosaurs covered the top of one medium sized bookshelf. A large assortment of books lined the shelves below and things that looked similar to flying birds with wheels. A computer, like the one Emily mentioned in the library, sat on the writing desk near the window.

"Now just stay in here. I'll be back soon. Pretend you're sleeping if anyone comes in the room. Voltar, are you listening to me?" she asked watching him look around the room.

"Miss Emily, there is so much to assimilate in this room. There are flying birds on wheels, a tiny tree baby and a miniature green woman standing on the tall dresser over there. What does your brother do with them and where are they from?" he asked touching the figurines.

"The birds, as you call them, are airplanes, the tiny tree boy is from a movie, and the green woman is an action figure."

"What action does she do? I have not seen her move."

"Never mind the toys. Do as I say or I'll have Sebastian drive us back to school and you can deal with trying to outrun the witch by yourself, is that clear?"

"Yes, Miss Emily, but what if the witch has followed us here? What are we going to do when she finds us?" he asked biting the side of his lip.

"We'll figure that out tomorrow."

"Can you get me that potion you spoke of so I can go out in the sunlight tomorrow?"

"The store is closed after dark," Emily responded. "We'll try to get it tomorrow."

"Miss Emily, do you truly have such a potion?" Voltar asked sounding somewhat skeptical. "Since, as you know, those of our kind cannot go outside in the daylight, why is the mixture not available at night? Am I a prisoner?" he asked.

"You're not a prisoner; we're just keeping you safe until we can get the potion, don't worry. Good night now," she said turning off the light. She left him alone in the room without ever answering his question about the made-up drug.

CHAPTER 10

Why Now?

Friday morning as Emily awoke, she heard voices. She pulled herself out of her comfortable and familiar bed to investigate. Quickly dressing, she peeked inside her brother's room, Zak and Voltar were still asleep in the twin beds. The mumbled voices came from right below Zak's room.

As she walked downstairs, she turned her head to the left. Sebastian lay sprawled out on the couch, asleep. At the bottom of the stairs, the voices grew louder; they came from the kitchen on her right. It sounded like her parents, arguing. They never argued; not even when she was little. Concerned, she stood by the door to listen.

"They can't stay here. It is too dangerous," her father said. "You know whose son that young man is."

"Where are they going to go Hugo? This is her home. We kept them apart to protect them, they were not supposed to meet, but it's too late now. They'll only be here until Sunday morning. It'll be fine until then. It's only a few short days."

Emily cracked the door open a sliver, spying on the exchange between her parents.

"Helen, I told you before they came, that I have a feeling *something* will happen. You know my feelings *always* come true," her father argued raising his voice. "We have to protect her from whatever it is. Asking her and him to leave is for their own safety. You know what it could be and we have Zak to think about."

"All right dear, I'll think of some excuse for them to leave after breakfast if you think that's best. You're scaring me, Hugo. We've never had a problem from *them,*" she said pointing upwards, "all these years. My only question is, why now?"

"Well something has happened, or about to happen, and they must go until we find out what. It's not safe here. I'll leave it to you to tell them after breakfast Helen," he stated.

Emily's hands shook as she stood by the door overwhelmed by the list of emotions she was feeling. Her father wanted her to leave and her mother was going along with his suggestion. Her entire world had turned upside down in that instant. Gathering her courage, she boldly walked into the kitchen, faking a smile.

"What's for breakfast?"

"Your father was just asking me the same question. He's about to go to the coop to see how many eggs the hens laid before I decide. Why don't you wake your friends and show them the farm while I make breakfast?" her mother said, not looking at her.

"Okay," Emily replied looking at the two of them intensely. "I love you both so much," she said giving both a huge hug. "I'll check on Voltar to see how he's doing and wake Zak."

Walking into the living room after her father left, she nudged Sebastian's shoulder and whispered, "Wake-up Sebastian. We have to talk, outside. I'll check on Voltar first," she said before turning to walk upstairs.

Opening Zak's door she saw Voltar standing over her brother's bed.

"What are you doing? You were sleeping a minute ago. Get back in bed," she whispered. "You're supposed to be sick."

Not moving a muscle Voltar said, "He snores. He snored all night, and loudly. I am hungry again just looking at him," he said rubbing his hands together. "I flew out the window last evening after everyone was asleep, and found a few small animals to quench my hunger, but I only took enough blood from them to stave off my hunger for a time. Do you think I can just—?"

"NO!" she growled before he had time to finish. "I'll get you some 'food' you *can* eat. Now get back in bed. If you touch my brother, we'll go back to the school, and I'll find the witch and let her take you. Now, get back in bed and pretend you're sleeping while I wake Zak."

After Emily pulled the shades down in the room, she woke Zak. "Voltar is sleeping, be quiet and get dressed. Mom's working on breakfast."

She went downstairs and told her mother Voltar was still sick and to let him sleep, then went into the living room.

"Come on Sebastian, we're going for a drive before breakfast," she ordered.

They drove in silence until reaching the end of the cornfield.

"Sebastian, something's wrong. My parents maybe a little strange, but they've started fighting since I've been away at school," she sniffled getting out of the car.

"There's a lot more wrong here than your parents, starting with your little vampire," he said slamming the car door while sidestepping her statement about her parents.

"Hiding out on this farm won't help, Emily. We have to go back to school Monday. We don't have the book to put Voltar or the witch back inside. What are we going to do?"

She sighed. "Look Sebastian, I don't have the answers either. That little boy has had a terrible life, and it's not his fault. I'm sure he just wants to go back home like any little boy."

"Emily, instead of being bossy like usual, you're being a tad soft-hearted when there's nothing we can do about Voltar's situation. For the safety of other people in our century, including us, the boy needs to go back inside the book. So far, we've been safe from the witch who's after him, and us I might add. How long do you expect it will take her before she catches up to us? She's a witch with powers, and what if Voltar finds out there is no 'special' drug?"

"You're right," she conceded, ignoring his crack about her being bossy. "So far we're safe, but what do you suggest we do? At this point I'll take any suggestion." Emily's eyes burned as she gazed at the cornfield across from the road. A single tear rolled down her cheek.

"What if that was my brother Zak, locked inside a book for centuries?" she moaned while staring at the field of corn. "I can't stand the thought of it Sebastian. I never believed in witches or the supernatural before yesterday. Have you read *anything* about getting rid of a witch before?"

"No. Only what I've seen on TV. The stuff on TV only showed what Voltar's already tried, like drowning or burning her. We tried running her over with a car and that didn't work either, according to Voltar."

Emily stared at the scarecrow in the cornfield while Sebastian talked. Its eyes seemed to follow her and its hand shifted a small degree.

"Did you see that?"

"Did I see what?" Sebastian asked.

Emily rubbed her eyes and looked again. The scarecrow's hand was in the same position as it had always been. When she was a little girl, the image of the straw man on the pole used to scare her.

Its faded red shirt, filled with holes and the overalls having only one strap buttoned, seemed almost comical now, not fearful. Even now, the weather-beaten buttons for eyes seemed to follower her. She shook off her old fear.

But old memories are powerful things.

"Never mind, it was just my imagination. I guess this whole thing has me creeped-out more than I thought. I could have sworn I saw the scarecrow's hand move. We'd better get back before breakfast is over or mom will check on Voltar. She'll open the shade in Zak's room and scream bloody murder when his skin begins to burn."

CHAPTER 11

The Witch and the Scarecrow

I t took all night for the witch to reach the forest near the farm. Riding on the skin and bone animal most of the way, one far past his prime, she was stiff and sore as she slipped off the creature at daybreak. The old deer was too fatigued and exhausted to go on. She left the worn-out creature, lying in the forest.

It was now the second day, and by tomorrow, her existence would end. She moved in the shadows of the forest, fearful of another trampling from the big metal box on wheels.

"I stink from riding that beast," she mumbled under her breath brushing off her clothes as she walked closer to the farm's cornfield. Her powers had dwindled even more during the night as each hour passed.

When she saw Emily and Sebastian drive up the dirt road and get out of the strange moving box, she hid behind a tree. She spotted a scarecrow that hung in the middle of the field and attempted to use her magic on it.

The scarecrow was too far away for her fading magic to

work. All it did was to allow him to flutter his hand like a fish flopping on dry ground. She silently watched when Emily and Sebastian drove away.

"They will pay for helping the boy to escape," she hissed as she came out of the woods.

It was easier in her weakened state to use an object that couldn't resist her magic. She had to get closer to the scarecrow if she had any hope to use it to get the boy back into the book before tomorrow.

"Come down from there," she ordered, pointing at the scarecrow as flashes of light flew from her fingertips.

The scarecrow moved slightly but looked to be stuck to the pole somehow. The witch walked around and untied the rope that secured him upright against the pole. She noticed a large spike piercing the back of his shirt holding him flat against the wooden beam tunneled deep into the ground. He remained fixed to the pole, without sliding down to the ground, as he should have.

Pointing her hand at the nail, she twisted her wrist and pulled back her finger slowly, causing the spike to bend and withdraw from the wood.

The scarecrow slid to the ground in a heap against the pole.

Its stuffing of straw with an old pillow in its chest, rearranged itself as he stood straight up on straw legs. The spell she cast on the scarecrow, had changed its appearance into a powerful-looking creature from a child's nightmare. The faded button eyes flashed an occasional white glow in the center. The smile once drawn on its face, now looked twisted, appearing wicked and evil as it waited for her command.

"Take me to the two witches who were here," she ordered.

The scarecrow lunged forward like a zombie caught in a trance. He followed the narrow dirt path with the witch trailing behind.

The old farmhouse was on a small hill along with a barn and chicken coop next to it. The metal box with wheels stood on the dirt road in front of the house.

Still frightened looking at the metal box that ran over her before, the witch grabbed the scarecrow's straw arm. "Bring the boy to me in the woods near the cornfield where you hung." She immediately left, not wanting to wait a moment longer. The two witches might have put some type of spell on the metal box to run her over again.

Zak finished breakfast and went out to play while waiting for Emily to come back. His mother said not to disturb Voltar until his sister and Sebastian returned. Bored with waiting, Zak snatched the pail his father used for worms and went behind the barn. He began digging, searching for large worms to use as bait for the fish in the pond nearby.

He was concentrating on his digging, while hoping to persuade his father to fish with him, if Voltar was still sick and couldn't play. A large shadow appeared over him. Without looking up, he started to tease his sister. "Hey sis, you're getting a little fat. Just look at your shadow," he taunted.

"Is Voltar better? Can I play with him now?" He grabbed the bucket and stood. When Zak turned, he froze, dropping the bucket on the ground. The scarecrow from the field loomed above his shorter body.

"Mom? Dad? Where are you?" he called out in a wavering small voice staring at the old scarecrow. Thinking for only a second, he announced, "Sis, this isn't funny, it's—freaky! Quit playing around, I'm telling mom and dad."

The scarecrow lowered his head as he reached out his arms to Zak. Zak promptly punched him in the stomach! "Your stomach's hard sis, like you stuffed the pillow with rocks but you're not fooling me. Take off the mask and show yourself or I'm marching into the house and telling mom how you tried to scare me like last Halloween. You'll be in big trouble."

He only had to wait a second for a response. The scarecrow picked Zak up and threw him over his shoulder, as he began to walk toward the woods.

"Okay, if you want to carry me around, go for it. Just don't throw me in the pond."

After what seemed like two or three minutes walking, Zak felt uncomfortable and began squirming. Upset over his sister carrying him like a sack of potatoes, he reached around to the side of the scarecrow's body and tried to pinch him. All he felt was the crunching of dried straw beneath the faded shirt. He moved his hand and squeezed the scarecrows body in different places. It all felt like...straw!

"Sis? Sis, are you in there?" he asked, trembling.

"Sis?"

The scarecrow's head swiveled around while still attached to his shoulders as he looked at Zak. Its eyes were shining at him while its painted mouth remained frozen in a creepy smile.

Zak's mouth dropped open before he passed out.

CHAPTER 12

Hostage

Zak dreamed he was on a boat rocking back and forth. Then he opened his eyes.

As he remembered where he was and what happened, a short chill of fear ran down his spine. The scarecrow was real and carrying him over its shoulder as the unearthly creature trudged toward the wooded area near the cornfield.

Zak began to thrash about in the scarecrow's arms. Panic set in when he couldn't free himself from the straw man's grasp. The straw crushed beneath his hands as he punched at the creature. Its arms began to squeeze tighter around him as he tried to escape.

"Help! Help!" Zak screamed. "Dad — Mom," he yelled. He screamed until he realized he was too far away from the house by now and they couldn't hear him.

The scarecrow swiveled his head all the way around, tightly twisting his neck like a rung out dishtowel, and looked at him.

Its creepy face, plastered with the eerie cloth smile, made him freeze and look away. Zak spotted the tree line ahead.

This has to be a dream, his young mind screamed in panic. *I have to wake up!*

Closing his eyes while forcing himself to relax, he figured once he calmed down he'd wake-up and it would all go away. He smelled the fragrance of pine trees in the woods, and felt the wind on his face. His eyes flashed open when a fly landed on his nose. He shooed it off. This was no dream and the scarecrow was alive.

When they had gone a few yards inside the forest, the scarecrow dropped Zak face down on the ground. He scrambled to his feet so he could run when a female voice behind him cackled. The scarecrow had blocked the only path of escape.

"Stay right there and turn around boy," the woman's voice commanded.

Fearing who or what stood behind him, he froze as a woman's hand touched his shoulder. Turning his head slightly to look over his shoulder, he saw a woman's hand. The wrinkled old hand, with knotty twisted knuckles, took hold of his shirt.

She tightened her grip on his shirt and swung him around with such force, he fell to the ground. As he got up and gathered his courage, he stood in front of her in a defiant stance with his hands on his hips while fighting the overwhelming feeling of fear.

He stood there waiting for her to speak. With his jaw clenched and his hands clutched into a fist, he fearlessly glared into her glowing green eyes.. She looked like an old hag with her shriveled face, crooked nose, and bent shoulders. She appeared to be like a witch in a book he once saw. The long black dress she wore flowed to the ground, covered in fresh dirt and holes.

The witch leaned over him, as if she was she inspecting her

captive. Her eyes widened as a surprised look washed over her face. "Who are you," the witch spat at him.

"Who are you!" Zak fired back. Not waiting for her answer, he went on. "Let go of me or I'll have my father call the police. When he finds out you've taken me, he's gonna be mad! He's big and strong."

"Shut up, little boy," she commanded as Zak opened his mouth once more to speak.

"He's —"

"Since you seem to be unable to be quiet," she interrupted, "I'll make you." The witch spread out her hand, and with a rapid swish of her wrist in front of his face, she shrieked, "Shut up!"

Zak coughed before he tried to speak, but no sound came out. He looked at her with rounded eyes and coughed again. Still, no words came out. His voice had vanished.

Streams of glowing light flew from the old woman's fingers to a large tree near him. The vines hanging down from the old tree wrapped themselves around his feet and arms. As the vines moved, they carried him up to a high barren spot on the tree's trunk. The tree's smaller limbs bent around him, locking him against the tree like a rope or chain.

"You will remain there and I will no longer need to put up with your incessant chattering, boy." She turned to look at the scarecrow who waited for her next command.

"You stupid creature," she shouted. "You brought me the wrong boy. Go back to that house, get me the other one, and be quick about it." She conjured up a large burlap bag and handed it to the scarecrow.

"Place the other boy at the farm inside this bag. He will burn to ashes in the sunlight and will be useless to me," she said. "My time is almost up and I only have one last surge of magic to use before my fate is sealed. Now go!"

CHAPTER 13

Blood Letting

Sebastian and Emily brought a plate of food to bring upstairs for Voltar after breakfast. They knew the vampire couldn't eat normal food, but they had to keep up appearances in front of her parents. When Emily pulled the covers back from over his head, Voltar appeared to be paler than normal, even for him, and honestly sick.

"Are you okay?" she asked.

"I've had no blood so I am growing weak," Voltar said, his voice sounding frail and soft. He looked at the food and turned away.

"I'll find you some. Can you drink chicken blood?" Emily asked.

He nodded yes.

"Come on Sebastian, sounds like we'll have chicken for dinner. Voltar, stay in bed until we come back," she said grabbing Sebastian's hand and running downstairs. She first grabbed a cup and a knife from the kitchen, and then nodded for Sebastian to follow her.

"We'll be back soon," Emily yelled back, walking out and closing the door behind her.

"Emily, even if we drain all the chicken's blood, it won't work," he said as they walked toward the chicken coop. "They only have about a tablespoon of blood in them. We need a larger animal."

She stopped and looked at him, raising her eyebrow. The memory of her father slaughtering a chicken for dinner during the former years came to mind. She decided what Sebastian said was true.

"So you're volunteering, right?" she stated folding her arms across her chest as she stopped walking.

"Me? Oh no, not me!" he said emphatically as he took a step back. "No, you're not blood-letting on me and besides, there are no doctors or equipment here."

"I've already given blood yesterday. It's, your turn. I'll just make a small cut on your arm and drain a small bit of your blood into this cup. Man up Sebastian."

Sebastian followed her back to the house. Inside, she walked him upstairs, holding his hand firmly.

After shutting the door to Zak's room, Emily pointed at her brother's bed. "Sit," she ordered Sebastian, "and hold out your arm."

Sebastian sat on the bed and squinted as he closed his eyes. He held out his arm and turned his head away, waiting for Emily to proceed. When she touched his arm, he flinched.

"If I bleed to death, it'll be your fault. Don't hurt me," he added. "I'll need stitches after you cut me and a doctor with antiseptic. I didn't hear you call a medic. An infection is a very probable reality especially if you cut an artery, then I might bleed to death. How far away is the nearest emergency room? Are you sure this is necessary?" he asked still keeping his eyes closed.

"You big baby," Emily replied. "It's already done; I did it while you were jabbering. I just need to grab a band-aid. Stay right there and hold this cup in your other hand," she said. "Zak keeps a few of them in his bedside drawer."

Reaching inside the drawer, she grabbed one and placed it over the cut. Afterward she handed the cup to Voltar and watched as he sipped it. Some coloring returned to his face.

"There, feel better?" Emily said as she touched Voltar's head and smiled down at the young vampire.

"Yes, but do I have to stay in this room? There is nothing to do lying in a bed. Have you secured the drug yet?"

"As I've told you before, the clinic is closed on weekends. We'll get it on Monday," she said turning around to face Sebastian as her eyebrows raised then lowered. "Don't take the band-aid off," she hissed, seeing him pick at it.

"We need to go downstairs before mom comes up. Voltar, I'll send Zak up here to play with you. Remember; don't mention you're being a vampire."

Walking into the kitchen where her mother was doing the dishes, Emily asked, "Mom, where's Zak? Voltar is feeling a little healthier and Zak asked when they could play together. I think a day spent inside playing would do them both good."

"He's out behind the barn, digging for worms again, I'm sure. I'm glad your friend's brother is feeling better."

"Yeah, thanks, so am I. Sebastian, talk to my dad while I get Zak."

Sebastian rolled his eyes at her before walking over to Mr. Paige.

"Good game yesterday, sir," Sebastian said. Though he himself never followed sport games, he knew most men did.

They were, in his opinion, a gigantic waste of time. Nevertheless, it was a subject, he was sure her father would waste a long time talking about. He wouldn't have to converse with him while he waited for Emily to get back.

"What game?" Mr. Paige asked him. "I think they're a waste of time on the farm. There are far more important things to do on a farm than to watch sport games," he answered coldly closing the Farmers Almanac magazine he had been reading for the weather forecast. He waited for the younger man's answer while staring straight at him.

Sebastian looked down. He shuffled over to the bookshelf appearing to look for a book as her father glanced down at the magazine and began to riffle through it once more. After he grabbed a book from the shelf and sat down, he thought, *Emily, hurry-up!*

Emily walked through the door a minute later without Zak. "Mom, he's not there, and he left the bucket half filled with dirt and worms drying out in the sun. Did he come back in?"

Sebastian, thankful she was back, rose from the couch.

"No. He's probably just hiding from you. Did you check in the barn or chicken coop?" her mother asked.

"Yes. I've checked everywhere. Does he have a new friend in the area?"

"No. Hugo, please go look for Zak. He's hiding from Emily," her mother said.

After a short time, her father returned without Zak. "I've searched and I can't find him. I told you Helen, something like this would happen. Now our son is missing."

"Calm down, he's not missing; he's just hiding," Emily said. "He's climbed a tree or something and is most likely sitting up there laughing at all of us. You stay here in case he comes back and Sebastian and I will go look for him."

"You don't understand, Emily," her father said shooting a

quick glance at his wife. "We've never told you our family secret."

"What secret? What do you mean?" she questioned denying the concern that abruptly flashed through her mind. She realized her fear over future events was about to come true. DIVORCE. A sudden anger rose in her she couldn't contain.

"Well, I figured out your little secret!" she shouted. "It's what you were arguing about in the kitchen this morning. You're getting a divorce. That's why you talked about having me leave today, before I found out. You wanted to keep your divorce hidden until it was over. I'm glad Zak's not here to hear this. I'm older and I can understand if that's the reason you want me to leave, but Zak is just a child and this will destroy him. You can't do it!"

"There are forces in this world looking for us Emily, and who want nothing more than to make us disappear," her mother whispered.

"Forces? Are you—," she hesitated for only a moment as she thought it over, "are you in some kind of trouble?" she asked gazing at her mother who appeared worried. "Who's looking for you? Are the police after you? What did you do?"

Mrs. Paige walked over, touched Emily's hand, and sighed.

"Dear, we're not getting a divorce, heaven's no! There's no easy way to tell you what I'm about to say." Mrs. Paige stole a glance at her husband before she continued.

"Your father is a wizard, and not just any wizard. He's the Grand Wizard of Warlocks. Others have been hunting him for a long time, so he can pass on his magic to one of them. We ran away and came to this century twenty years ago to have a normal life, and to give you a normal life, too. They are after us and may have taken your brother to force our return."

Emily laughed. "That's the big family secret? My father is a wizard. Mom, get real, I'm not a child and I don't read fairy tales or believe in dragons and wizards."

"Emily!" her father thundered. "Your mother is telling you the truth."

CHAPTER 14

The Truth Comes Out

Emily's mouth dropped.

After first sitting in her father's favorite chair, a stunned Emily asked, "A wizard! Are you both crazy?"

"Now dear, don't 'freak out' as the kids say these days," her mother began. "We ran away from the High Court for a peaceful life together. There are many dangers at court. We vowed to protect you from the courts harmful influence and the assassins there. Your father only went back a few times to get something we needed."

"Never mind all of that, Helen," Mr. Paige said. "We can explain it to her later. We need to find Zak."

Sebastian walked over to Emily and whispered through his teeth, "Did he say he was a wizard, or am I hallucinating?"

"Shut up, Sebastian!" she screamed jumping up from the chair. "Give me a minute to think."

"We don't have time to waste while we talk it over. Zak could be in grave danger," her father said walking toward the door.

"Wait-a-minute!" Emily yelled. She ran to the door and held

up her hands to stop him from leaving. "There's a witch chasing us, a vampire upstairs, and now you're telling me," she said glaring at her father, "you're a wizard?" she stated sounding half-crazy. "Is that right?"

"I believe that is what he said," Voltar offered walking down the stairs. "But, whether your father is a wizard, only you can know. Now, I am supposed to be resting according to your wishes Miss Emily, which I cannot do with all the screaming down here." Voltar waited on the bottom stairs for her answer.

"What witch and what vampire?" her father demanded, glancing at the group.

"Him," Sebastian said pointing to Voltar. "He's the vampire. I don't know what witch, except that she came out of a book Emily opened in the library. Voltar came out first. After that, I guess the witch came out while we left to get blood for him," Sebastian offered. "I ran Voltar's witch over with my car when she ran after us in the auditorium, but Voltar told us she's still alive."

"I am confident she has found a way, to follow us here," Voltar offered.

Mr. Paige raised an eyebrow. "Emily, the answer to your question is yes, I am a wizard." Mr. Paige glanced away a second and then stared at his wife. "Is it possible? Have they both become what we feared?" he asked his wife before darting his eyes quickly at Emily and Sebastian.

He turned to Sebastian. "Both came out of a book that Emily opened when *you* were with her?" he questioned. "Is that correct?" he asked waiting for Sebastian's reply.

"Yes."

Mrs. Paige slipped her hand over her mouth and raised her eyebrows, in surprise. "Is it possible that Emily and Sebastian are—?" she asked, never finishing her sentence while staring at her husband.

He ignored her question.

"It has to be Alizon," Mr. Paige said a moment later. "She owned the shop in London. A few days ago, I conducted business with her. There was a disagreement and I cursed her. Nasty woman."

"If Alizon took our son, she's dangerous Hugo, you know that," his wife said as she lowered her head and looked down.

"Does she have the Book?" Mr. Paige asked ignoring his wife's concern.

"I don't think so, but she could have gone back and gotten it," Sebastian replied. "Why?"

"If she is who I think she is, she needs Voltar, and the Book," her father said turning toward the vampire. "How did she imprison you inside that book to begin with Voltar?"

"With a charm she gave me that stunk like dung," he answered wrinkling his nose. "Your daughter and her friend tried to help me and now your son is missing, most likely taken by her. I am sorry, sir."

"I know that spell, it's a nasty one and hard to break. Alizon has a bad reputation for being tricky and only she can break it. I rarely use my powers, so my ability in a battle against her may be off a bit."

"So sir, are you able to undo the—?"

"Voltar, go into the kitchen and be quiet!" Emily shouted at the young vampire before he finished.

"You need not yell, I possess excellent hearing," Voltar calmly said leaving the room.

"Dad, do you think Zak went into the cornfield?" Emily asked. "I didn't check there."

"He likes the woods near the field," her mother offered. "Hugo, do you think he'd hide there, or do you believe Alizon took him? It might be someone from the council who's taken him."

"If it was the council, they would have notified us by now. No, it's not them," he answered. "Zak's hiding, or the witch grabbed him by mistake."

Mr. Paige's eyes darted about the room before he spoke. "The vampire boy can't go outside, it's still daylight. Alizon knows that so she won't come until dark. But the field is large and it will take me a long time to search it alone, possibly until dusk."

"I have a car, we can drive there and look together," Sebastian offered.

"No, we might miss him if he's taken the shortcut leading to the cornfield," Mrs. Paige said. "I think Emily and I should walk down the path to the field, while you and Sebastian take the road to the woods." She touched her husband's arm. "Hugo, what if it is the witch who has him?"

"She will regret it, I assure you, my dear," he said patting her hand before he turned around toward Emily. "Instruct him to stay here," he said glancing at Voltar, "while we search for Zak. If Zak returns before we get back, he and Zak must hide from the witch inside the house."

She nodded and stuck her head inside the kitchen door. Not seeing the vampire at the table, she stepped into the room and looked in the large pantry to tell him to wait until they returned. Then she called out. "Voltar, where are you?" she questioned.

No response came.

Noticing the back door wide open, she assumed her mother accidentally left it open. She picked up a piece of straw from the floor as she closed the door. Knowing the vampire wouldn't have gone outside since it was sunny, she forcefully said, "Voltar, this isn't funny. Where are you hiding? Come out this instant."

No answer.

She marched into the living room. "Dad, he's not in the kitchen. He must have gone upstairs. Mom, you left the back door open again," she stated.

"I did not," her mother protested. "I never even went out the door; I was doing the dishes from breakfast.

"Well, he couldn't have gone outside," Emily said.

"Go check Zak's room," her father suddenly said. "If you don't find him in Zak's room, check the rest of the rooms upstairs. We'll look down here, don't forget to check the bathroom, he's got to be here somewhere," her father directed.

After a quick search, Emily came back downstairs. "He's not up there."

Her father noticed the straw still in her hand. Holding out his open hand, a silent request to give it to him, he examined the single piece of straw.

"Where did you get this?" he asked.

"It was on the kitchen floor."

"This," he said, raising the straw to eye level in front of them, "is not just a piece of straw. It's from the old scarecrow in the field by the age and feel of it. The witch is here and now has both boys," he stated.

"I'm guessing she sent the scarecrow to take the vampire boy, and he took Zak by mistake. She has them both now and needs to get the vampire back into the book. I don't know what she'll do to Zak, and that scares me."

"Why would she dare to keep Zak if you're the Grand Wizard?" Emily asked a little skeptical over such an idea.

"I was the one who cast her into the book on my last visit because she tried to cheat me. If she has her spell book already, she'll cast a spell over Zak," Mr. Paige said. "Her temper is well-known and her anger knows no bounds. I pray she doesn't recognize me or that it was I who cast her into the book."

"Wait a minute," he clamored taking off for the stairs. "I have to get a few things before we find them."

CHAPTER 15

The Witch and the Wizard

M r. Paige ran upstairs to his bedroom. Lifting an oak floorboard near a dresser, he reached under it and took out two items. One was a short piece of ebony wood and the other, a long purple robe with ancient writing on it. After putting the garment on, he inhaled a deep breath and starred at the wooden stick for only a second before leaving the room.

He hurried down the stairs two at a time, with the twenty-four inch stick in his hand.

"Dad, what are you wearing and what's that stick for?" Emily asked, meeting him at the bottom of the stairs.

"It's what I need to confront the witch when we find her. I'm assuming she used our scarecrow to grab both boys and took them to the woods. There's no other place for her to hide nearby except in the woods. I don't know which path the scarecrow took, but I'm sure he's taken him to where she is."

"We won't need to split up if we get there first," Sebastian stated, looking at Mr. Paige. "If we take my car we'll be able to find where the witch is hiding, before the scarecrow gets there with Voltar."

"Right! The car is faster," Mr. Paige agreed. "Let's go."

The men jumped into the front seat of the car with Emily and her mother in the backseat. Parking behind a bush near the cornfield, they sat and waited for the scarecrow to arrive with Voltar.

Soon they spotted the scarecrow shuffling along the alternate path with an old burlap bag slung across his shoulder.

"Look!" Mrs. Paige shrieked looking out the car's window. "The bag is moving."

"He's got Voltar inside the bag!" Emily shouted, reaching for the car door handle, ready to sprint out of the car.

"Wait until we see the witch," her father commanded giving Emily a sharp harsh look he used when she was a child.

"Helen, when the witch emerges, you and Emily go find Zak and the vampire boy. Sebastian, you will drive all of them back to the house while I deal with Alizon, alone. Do you all understand the plan?" her father asked turning back, watching the woods for the witch.

"I'm fine with staying in the car," Sebastian murmured under his breath.

An aged woman with scraggly hair wearing a long, frayed black dress slowly emerged from the woods.

She looked nothing like the woman Emily and Sebastian encountered at the library. "That's not the woman who chased us," Sebastian said. "She was much younger and wore a suit. I don't think that's the witch."

"It's the witch," Mr. Paige said in a low voice. "She can't keep up the disguise she used when you saw her at the school. The spell she cast on her appearance to fool you drained too much of her power. She has only enough for one last surge of power available, and she plans to use it to get the boy back into the book."

The witch's back was toward the car when she walked out of the woods to meet the scarecrow.

"Everybody out, it's time," Mr. Paige said lifting the door handle. "Sebastian, you come with me. We'll need to distract the witch while Helen and Emily grab the boys." Emily's father was out of the car first with Sebastian slowly following.

"Hey Alizon, you old hag, where's my son?" Mr. Paige demanded as Sebastian stood beside him a distance away.

The witch turned and saw both Mr. Paige and Sebastian coming toward her. Narrowing her eyes at Emily's father she said, "You don't know my power or what I can do to you. Stand back, both of you, or you'll regret it."

"Remember who I am witch, and what I am capable of. For the last time, where is my son?" Mr. Paige demanded as he and Sebastian moved closer.

"You're the one who cast me inside the book!" the witch cried as her face distorted in anger. "Your son will pay the price for that!"

Emily and her mother silently moved toward the tree line when the scarecrow entered the woods. They scanned the area for Zak while her father kept the witch talking.

The witch's eyes focused on Emily and her mother as they entered the forest of trees. Alizon shot a quick look at the trees and mumbled an incantation under her breath. The trees began to shake and pick up their roots as they began to move, until they formed a tight circle around them and the scarecrow.

Standing inside the encircling trees, Emily looked up as the shadows from the trees, began to hide the sunlight. When she looked up, she also saw Zak trapped against a tree trunk high above her, waving his only free arm. The tree's boughs squeezed tighter around Zak as he struggled to free himself.

"Zak, we'll get you down, give us a minute," Emily shouted. She noticed his mouth moving, but no words came out. "He can't speak, what's wrong with him, mom?"

"Emily, the witch cast a spell over his vocal cords so he couldn't call out for help. I have to tell your father before it's too late for him to undo," Mrs. Paige said. She ran to a small separation between the trees. "Hugo," she yelled out, "the witch put a spell on Zak. He's stuck in a tree and can't speak."

Alerted to his son's condition, Mr. Paige immediately pulled the stick from his pocket and aimed it at the tree. The tree released its grip on Zak.

Zak floated twelve feet down from the tree into Emily's arms.

The witch mumbled a command at the scarecrow who promptly hung the burlap bag he was holding on a broken limb on one of the trees. He moved toward Emily, her mother, and Zak.

Voltar shouted from the bag, "Miss Emily, is that your voice I hear?"

"Yes, but stay inside the bag, Voltar. It's daylight. We have a situation here and you're safer inside there. Don't try to come out," Emily shouted while she and her mother kept Zak behind them and away from the scarecrow.

The witch glanced at the area and muttered another spell. All types of crawling things from the forest began moving, heading toward Mr. Paige and Sebastian. It looked like an army moving under a blanket. All manner of spiders, ants, cockroaches and underground insects, crept toward them.

"Mr. Paige! Mr. Paige, do you see what's coming?" Sebastian screeched, terrified of the crawling things heading over a small mound in the dirt as they advanced toward them. He moved closer to Mr. Paige. "Can you do something about them?" he said pointing at the creatures.

"I'm a bit busy boy trying to remember incantations. Leave me alone!" Mr. Paige roared.

"Take that," the witch shouted, flicking her finger at Mr. Paige. A flash of brilliant orange light shot toward him as the skies darkened from the magical battle occurring below. He moved out of the way and shot a jolt from his wand toward her. It blasted a yellow stream of light in her direction, completely missing her.

"Can't you do better than that?" Sebastian asked. "You missed the witch by a mile and the crawly things are almost here."

"I haven't battled a witch in a long time. Just shut up boy and stand back."

"Hugo, could you hurry up, we can't keep dodging this scarecrow," his wife yelled through the trees. "Fix Zak's voice while you're at it," she added. They kept zigzagging through the circle of trees away from the scarecrow, keeping Zak behind them, out of the scarecrow's reach.

Mr. Paige, concentrating on his aim, shot a well-placed flame hitting the scarecrow in between the trees. The scarecrow easily caught on fire and started to burn. Sparks of burning straw flew upward, spreading to the trees. The smell of burning wood and smoke filled the air as the dried trees began to quickly burn around them.

"They're getting closer," Sebastian shrieked to Mr. Paige as he crushed an advancing roach. "You're supposed to be some Grand Wizard, so do something!" he hollered as his voice picked up speed and beads of sweat covered his forehead.

Mr. Paige, exchanging volts of energy with the witch, paid no attention to him.

"Hugo, help!" Emily's mother screamed in the distance as dried tree branches began to fall.

Fire from the tightly clustered trees grew hotter. Black smoke rose high above the trees as the fire raged. Within seconds, the fire began to consume all the oxygen within the circle of trees.

Gasping for air and coughing through the smoke, she called out again, "Hugo, help."

Sebastian, petrified by the insects and small creatures climbing over his shoes, he took off running. He plowed smack into the witch from the side like a linebacker, knocking her over as he tried to get away from the bugs.

He kept running, until he stood outside the circle of burning trees where Emily and the others remained trapped inside. Panic washed over his face, as he watched Emily and her mother gasping for air inside the fire ring. They will suffocate and burn to death in the firestorm if he doesn't do something.

An adrenaline rush filled his veins. He grabbed the smallest tree in the circle and with supernatural strength, uprooted it completely, and threw it aside.

"Emily!" he called out through the circle of burning trees, "come this way."

After helping Mrs. Paige and Zak through the tree opening, Sebastian saw Emily turn to run back. He grabbed her arm, pulling her out.

"Voltar's inside the bag," she said, coughing and pointing at the burlap bag hanging on the limb.

"Stay here," he ordered. Running back into the burning inferno, he grabbed the bag with Voltar inside and hoisted it over his shoulder. With his eyes burning from the intense smoke, he ran toward the opening, dodging burning tree branches falling around him. Sebastian slid out the small opening with the vampire in the bag slung over his shoulder.

The witch's eyes narrowed as she watched him run toward the car holding the bag with her vampire boy inside.

Mr. Paige used the opportunity to shoot a massive bolt at the witch, knocking her to the ground, stunning her for a moment. The magic she used on the trees and bugs stopped instantly, as she lay dazed.

Mr. Paige walked over to the witch and pulled her halfway up from the ground as Emily and the others reached the car.

"Take the spell off my son or I'll kill you where you lay."

Her eyes scanned the area for anything to use against the wizard. Spying a large cindered tree limb on the ground, she moved her finger as the wizard glared into her eyes.

The broken charred limb flew behind him, smashing against his head before it fell to the ground. He dropped onto one knee, releasing his hold on the witch.

"Dad!" Emily screamed watching the horrific scene as he fell to the ground.

Alizon stood and shot a small sparkling flame at him. The flash from her finger fell short of its mark looking like a sparkler instead.

Hearing his child's scream, he shook his head, to clear it from the impact of the limb, and shot one powerful bolt at the witch, knocking her to the ground again.

"Alizon, you will regret that," he stated getting up. "Do what I ordered or die right here."

Forced to give up knowing her powers had dwindled to almost nothing, she use the last of her power to remove the spell she cast on Zak's vocal cords, and then turned toward Mr. Paige, "Who *are* you?"

"I am the Grand Wizard and you shall do no more harm to my family." He slowly waved his wand in a circle, causing thunder and lightening to break through the skies. A turning of his wrist caused a cloud of whirling darkness to descend over her.

Alizon shuddered, terrified by what was to come. "Are you going to kill me?" she whined as the cloud surrounded her, trapping her inside. The whirlwind rose off the ground with the witch inside, screaming and cursing. She vanished before their eyes.

Emily clung to Sebastian as they stood outside the car. Breaking away for a minute, he placed the bag with Voltar inside the car.

When her father came towards them, Emily ran to him. After a long hug, she looked into his eyes.

"I need some answers to, I don't know, a million questions?" she said.

"Of course you do," Mr. Paige said putting an arm around his wife. "Let's go home, get cleaned-up, have a cup of tea, and then I'll answer as many as possible."

CHAPTER 16

All is Revealed

"We're home now, so talk father and tell me what's going on," Emily demanded as Sebastian released Voltar from the bag.

Looking at the group covered in ash and smelling like smoke, Mr. Paige shook his head. "Helen, would you make us some tea? This will be a lengthy discussion."

"Yes dear, but showers first, everybody," her mother announced while pinching her nose.

After an hour of taking showers and washing the grime off, they met downstairs. Emily showered and put on clean clothes, while Sebastian wore a fresh shirt from her father and sat on the couch. Voltar, seated on the stairs, wore the clothes he wore when he came out of the book. The group marched into the kitchen.

Mrs. Paige poured the tea when it was ready, as the group sat at the kitchen table waiting for the discussion to begin. Her father spoke.

"Emily, we hoped you and your brother would never find out about our 'special ability'. As your mother said before, we ran away from the council because we wanted you to have a normal life, but it is apparent now, that it only put you in danger."

"Because Sebastian's father is from a long line of warlocks and I am the Grand Wizard of our clan, it was conceivable that you both may have powers. Your mother and Sebastian's mother, have no powers, so we hoped you not to have them and could lead a simple normal life.

"You displayed no special powers while you grew up and we felt our fear was for naught. By the time you reached the age of eighteen, if you had them, any proximity to a magical object would activate them. That's the reason we sent you off to college, Emily. Without magic around, you would be safe. After you met each other and touched the Magical Book, it triggered both your powers to awaken.

"Sebastian's family came with us to be free of the council's influence. We moved away from each other to protect both of our families and left behind all magical items, except the ones under the floorboard in the bedroom. We stopped you from going into our room, Emily, for that reason. If you came near my wand, your powers, if you had any, would activate when you were a young child. Then we did our best to keep you both safe by keeping you apart."

"Excuse me a minute," Sebastian interrupted. "Did you just say, my father is a warlock?"

"Yes, it's in your long bloodline. That's why you could uproot that tree and free the others. After I figured out whose son you were, I notified your parents early this morning. They are on their way here. It will be a fine reunion; they should be here by dinner."

Zak, quiet since his encounter with the witch, started jabbering. "This is so cool! I am the son of a wizard and my father is the Grand Wizard, not just a simple farmer. Am I magical, too, dad?"

"Son, there is nothing shameful in being a farmer. It is what I chose when we came. We contribute to this world by feeding many others. I am proud to be a farmer; it's a worthy occupation. We don't know if you have any powers," he said. Under his breath he whispered, "I hope not, for the world's sake."

"Remember Zak, you can't tell anyone. It would put us all in danger," his father added. "And there's the matter of you, Emily, being a witch. Since opening the Book, your powers will grow, but there is a danger using them. The council will know and hunt you down until they find you, then demand you go back. They will not allow our family to remain here."

"Emily," Mrs. Paige said, "the council did not approve of our marriage when they found out. They demanded we divorce and your father marry another, so we ran away to be together. If we were to go back, they would imprison me for disobedience. The council is not forgiving. I don't know what they would do to your father, but they would administer a punishment of some sort because of our actions."

Emily starred at her mother as tears formed in her eyes. Her parents love surpassed any she ever read in a book, even Romeo and Juliet's love.

"Where did you send the witch or did you kill her?" Voltar asked.

"No, I didn't kill her; I sent her to a place she loved to visit. I sent her into the Book," her father said smiling, "without her powers."

"And what about me?" he asked. "Will you still give me the drug so I no longer am a vampire?" he asked turning to Emily..

"I'm sorry to tell you there is no drug, Voltar," Emily said looking down. "Sebastian and I told you that so you wouldn't harm others for the blood you needed. Dad, is there something you can do to help Voltar?"

Mr. Paige watched as the young vampire's head dropped in sadness.

"Voltar, I cannot change you back into a human. I am truly sorry. I need you to answer some questions to see what I can do. Okay?"

"Yes sir," the young vampire answered softly.

"When you were turned, where were you and what were you doing?"

"I ran to get some bread for my mother at dusk, but before I got to the bakery shop, a man approached me asking for directions. I showed him the way to the street he should take when he pulled me into an alley and attacked me."

"Someone walked by and interrupted the vampire before he killed me. He left me for dead. I went into the witches shop the next day for a charm and she imprisoned me inside the book."

"So no one knew about the attack except the witch. Is that correct?" Mr. Paige asked.

"That is correct, sir. Only the witch knew what I was when I went to her shop for the charm."

Mr. Paige sat back in thought rubbing his chin. "There is one thing I can do," he stated, "if you would like to give it a try."

"I will accept anything you can do," Voltar said, "except being turned into a bug," he added in a low tone looking down.

Those around the table chuckled, even Mr. Paige.

"What I can do is send you back in time to the day *before* you were turned. You will remember everything from your experience here, but you may never mention what happened there or here, to anyone, or the spell will be reversed."

"You mean I can be with my mother again and not a vampire? The thirst will go away?"

"Yes."

"Can you do it right away, sir?" the little vampire asked. "Wait!" Voltar shouted. "I must say good-by to all of you and thank you for your kindness to me. You have accepted me and protected me. I cannot thank any of you enough. Not many people would help a stranger who is a—vampire. I will pray for you all my days, and go to church as my mother asked. I will—,"

"It's okay Voltar," Emily interrupted walking over to him. "Just give me a hug."

Voltar shook hands with the others as he thanked them individually, his bright blue eyes shining with pent up tears. He then turned toward Mr. Paige.

"I am ready sir."

Emily's father waved his wand. Voltar slowly disappeared into a mist as he waved good-by.

Sebastian's parents arrived for dinner at dusk. They talked about old times for hours. As soon as dinner was over, Emily suggested she and Sebastian take a walk. Once away from the house, she turned and faced him.

"You saved me from the fire, why?" she asked looking up at him, while taking off his glasses. She stared into his pewter colored eyes.

"I don't know," he said trying to change the subject but not able to turn away. "What—what do we do now, knowing we're *special* I mean?" he asked quickly, having no answer for what he felt except an awkwardness.

"We'll go back to school and come back on the weekends to find out more about how 'special' we are," she said smiling up at him.

She wrapped her arms around him and she kissed him, long and slow. A smiled crossed his lips as they broke apart.

Zak, hiding nearby, had followed them outside. He heard them talk about having 'special powers'. *'I wonder what powers I have. This is going to be a fun year!'*

ABOUT THE AUTHOR

Korra Grey is an emerging author that loves to write action comedies for her grandchildren. After writing her first book she was urged to publish it.

Now that she's figured it all out, she looks forward to writing a lot more.

Not to mention her grandkids are demanding to read Zak's story.

www.ingramcontent.com/pod-product-compliance
Lightning Source LLC
Chambersburg PA
CBHW070804120626
46557CB00002B/711